While the other children are . cosy beds at the abandoned hospit. practise for the performance of a lij the air, a sudden 'interruption' leaves her in terrible pain setting a chain of events crashing into motion. With only days to go until the mysterious inhabitants of the abandoned hospital step centre stage, a replacement must be found, and fast! But who on earth can backflip into such talented shoes at such short notice? Cucumber thinks she can! The youngest of the troupe she has been secretly studying the routine for weeks and is certain she's the obvious choice. Unfortunately, Mrs M, aka 'The Boss', has other ideas…

Meanwhile, on the other side of town, wannabee magician Edward and his younger brother Nicky are enjoying the summer holidays blissfully unaware that Nicky is about to disappear! Luckily, with their mother away on a business trip and the telly-loving au pair dreaming of romance, Edward might just have enough time to find him before anyone notices he's gone…

In his quest, Edward turns detective, following a confusion of clues as he desperately searches for his little brother. Along the way, he encounters a cast of characters who help and hinder him in equal measure. From a postcard-licking puppy to a strange little old lady called Mrs Cabbage and the argumentative Grouchers.

Elsewhere Nicky begins to wonder whether he has made the most terrible and terrifying decision ever!

DISAPPEARING ACT

This story is dedicated to

anyone who has ever wanted

to go on an adventure...

ISBN 978-1-9163201-0-9 (paperback)

Chapter One
Disastrous Start

With the show only days away, Cassie was feeling nervous and excited. Although confident with the routine, she wanted her first performance in front of an audience to be perfect so she woke early and dressed in her favourite red tracksuit. The other children were still fast asleep, so hurriedly, she pigtailed her abundance of dark, chocolate-brown coloured locks and wiggled her feet into a pair of tatty gym shoes. Then, slipping silently from the dormitory, she made her way through the abandoned hospital.

Along the crumbling corridors she tiptoed, dancing this way and that, trying to avoid the dusty blackened cobwebs that hung from the ceiling and brushed against her face. The adults had left this side of the vast building to fall into disrepair. Water puddled on the cracked vinyl where it dripped from the leaky ceiling and dribbled down the walls.

Cassie much preferred the clean and cosy corner they lived in on the other side of the old hospital. Over there it didn't smell of mouldy mushrooms and damp dog.

As she reached the huge doors of the operating room, Cassie hesitated before tentatively placing her hand on the cool, white surface. She hated the windowless room; it was creepy and cold but perfect for the routine, providing her with enough space and height to practise.

Bravely, she pushed the door and felt in the darkness for the light switch, waiting while the bright tubes of brilliant white buzzed and flickered into life. Now fully lit, the room glared at her as she imagined the shiny tiles reflecting the operations once performed within its walls; fingers stitched, ears syringed and boils lanced. The images made her shudder, but with no time to lose she scrubbed them from her mind and began.

Leaping and flying high above the ground, Cassie somersaulted, flipped and spun this way and that, repeating the moves over and over until finally, catching her breath, she filled a plastic cup with water. The cool liquid flushed down her throat, streaming its way into her tummy and a satisfying chill ran through her. She refilled the cup and began glugging once more, only stopping when a strange yawning sound echoed softly around the room.

Cassie listened while her eyes searched, coming to rest on a stack of chairs in the far corner. Inching forwards nervously, she'd only taken a few steps when another sound interrupted her, a sound far more menacing, far more alarming than the first. It was the low droning hum of Mrs M's vacuum cleaner. Cassie knew The Boss wasn't interested in the neglected operating theatre and never cleaned this side of the building; she'd simply come to interfere.

The young girl leapt into position and was mid-jump when the noise increased and the vacuum barged into the room, closely followed by Mrs M. Cassie dreaded her arrival and the inevitable disapproval that would follow. No doubt her performance would be picked apart and every minor mistake criticised.

Meanwhile, inside the stack of chairs, Cucumber, the youngest of the children, stifled another yawn and shuffled back to avoid getting caught. She'd been spying on Cassie all morning, scribbling furiously in her picture diary where little figures now filled the page. Desperate to be as good as the older girl, she hadn't wanted to miss a single arm-stretch or leg-bend and definitely didn't want to get discovered. So, with Cassie in full flight, Cucumber returned to her drawing, determined not to get distracted by Mrs M's grumbling. The Boss complained about everything all the time and, to begin with, the little girl had no problem ignoring her. However, as the vacuum reached the far corner, it began to splutter and whine. Alarmed, Cucumber peered out as Mrs M started tugging at the machine ferociously. Things then went from bad to worse as it entered a final deathlike scream, followed by Mrs M's own ear-splitting cry.

"**AAAAAGGGGHHHH!** I can't believe it! I told Bernard to check it weeks ago, now look, it's useless!" she spat furiously.

Cassie tried to help.

"It's not broken, Mrs M, it's just caught on the…"

But it was too late!

There was a *FIZZ!*

Followed by a **FLASH!**

And finally, a **BANG!**

The chairs came crashing down as the room filled with smoke and the plug from the vacuum cleaner started shooting out flames. An explosion of dust, fluff and dead skin rocketed from the machine, covering them in a gritty grey substance.

Bernard rushed in, his grey, bushy eyebrows waggling up and down in agitation.

"Quick! Quick!" screamed Mrs M. "The place is about to go up in flames, don't just stand there, you old fool, do something!"

"What happened?" he cried, racing around in a tearing hurry still holding the plate of cheese sandwiches he'd brought for Cassie.

"The plug! The plug!" she yelled. "It's on fire!"

Bernard glanced over to where Mrs M pointed, but instead of tackling the plug, he hastily rushed out leaving the doors of the operating room flapping backwards and forwards.

"What are you doing now?" she bellowed, chasing after him.

Hot on his heels, she'd almost reached the doors when they suddenly swung open again and the plate of sandwiches hurtled through the air, spinning towards her head like a frisbee. Stumbling backwards, Mrs M lost her footing and landed on her bottom. Bernard, already halfway across the room when he heard the thud, was too desperate to stop the old hospital burning to the ground, so ignored it. Luckily, by the time he reached the plug, it had stopped sparking.

"Electricity's off!" he gasped. "Emergency over!"

Mrs M scrabbled back onto her feet and, catching Bernard by surprise, loomed out of the smoke, her face twisted with rage.

"Emergency over?!" she shrieked. "I told you it needed fixing!"

Bernard looked into her wild eyes and decided not to argue.

"I think you'd better have a lie down my dear, I'll see to Cassie and come and check on you later."

Mrs M stalked furiously from the room while Bernard hurried over to the young girl.

"My little darling, whatever happened?" he asked, examining her carefully.

"Mrs M caught the lead from the vacuum cleaner on the chairs and when she yanked it free, they toppled over and hit me."

By now, the pain was increasing and her eyes prickled with tears.

"My arm hurts, and my leg," she gasped.

"I don't think you've broken anything," replied Bernard, trying to reassure her, "but you'll need some bandages."

"Oh Bernard, no! What about Friday?"

Cassie looked at him, tears now trickling down her cheeks, as she realised the routine she'd spent months perfecting would be impossible to perform.

"Never mind about the show, let's find Aunty H and the first aid kit, she'll sort you out."

With pain shooting through her limbs, Cassie held on tightly as Bernard helped her limp from the room.

Once they'd gone, and with the dust settled, Cucumber emerged from the tangled mess of chairs and brushed herself down. Taking a few steps towards the middle of the room she bowed and, imagining the cheering audience, blew kisses and waved to their admiring faces. Then, opening the picture diary, she traced the figures with her finger and her tummy backflipped as a wave of excitement washed over her.

Positive that none of the other children knew the routine, she couldn't wait for the moment The Boss would ask her to step in. 'Cucumber, there's been an unfortunate accident. Cassie won't be able to perform on Friday night, you're the only one who can save the day!'

The little girl giggled and her eyes sparkled as a huge smile spread across her face.

For Saol

Chapter Two

Trampoline

Inside Number 8, Apple Blossom Crescent, Nicky Dealer backflipped off the end of his bed onto the soft grey carpet. Number 8, where Nicky lived, was identical to all the other houses. Towering, three-storey red brick buildings separated by fences. In front, paved driveways parked shiny modern cars while huge gardens, big enough for swimming pools and trees, spread out behind.

Perched on top of a hill, Apple Blossom Crescent looked down into the valley where Station Road snaked through the shops in the centre of town. It was much busier below with the hustle and bustle of people buying everyday stuff, only becoming quieter as the road continued onwards, past the old hospital. In the distance, if Nicky looked hard enough, he could see the top of the leafy, overgrown trees that shielded the crumbling hospital building and, if he looked even harder, the high stone wall that surrounded it. But he never looked. He never looked because everything he wanted was right in front of him and as a keen gymnast, he had more than enough space. He really was a fortunate little boy.

The summer holidays had just begun and that morning, as soon as he'd woken, he'd cartwheeled across the landing into his older brother's bedroom. With his birthday only a week away he'd finally decided what he wanted.

"Edward!" he shouted, spinning into the room. "Are you awake?"

"Mmm mmm," came the mumbled reply from the brown mop of hair that poked out of the bedcovers.

"Great, I need to speak to you."

His brother didn't reply.

"Ed!" Nicky yelled while launching into a handstand and walking around the room on his hands.

Edward pulled the covers down, feeling for his glasses

on the bedside table.

"Morning Nicky, you okay?" he asked, tilting his head to one side and trying to focus on his upside-down brother.

"Oh, I am Ed. I had the most amazing dream."

Nicky flipped back onto his feet, wiping his shaggy blonde hair from his eyes.

"It was brilliant. I was bouncing on clouds like they were trampolines and I want to ask Mummy to get me one."

"A cloud?" teased Edward while yawning.

"No! A trampoline!" replied Nicky, a note of frustration sounding in his voice. "Where is she?"

"Sorry Nicky, Mummy's going away on an important business trip so she won't have time for you to ask her today, but she'll be back tomorrow, it'll have to wait until then."

Edward pulled himself out of bed as Nicky's shoulders drooped disappointedly. He wished his mother wasn't always so busy. Her company, Dealer & Sons, found work for actors, celebrities and pop stars who, she said, were more demanding than children. That meant, as she catapulted from one business meeting to the next, the incapable Claudette cared for them.

Unsuited to being an au pair, Claudette had originally plodded into Mrs Dealer's office in search of something that would make her famous, but seconds into the audition it became abundantly clear she had absolutely no talent. Luckily, Mrs Dealer desperately needed help and with nothing to fall back on, Claudette had accepted on the spot. So, while the boys entertained themselves, she spent hours in front of the television, dreaming of becoming a star.

Nicky stood for a moment, pondering the size and colour of the trampoline he'd ask for while picking his nose and eating the bogey.

"Shall I get breakfast?" Edward chuckled. "You seem hungry!"

Nicky grinned sheepishly before wiping his finger on his pyjama top.

"Okay," he said, pushing past and sprinting towards the stairs. "Last one down's a stinky egg!"

In the kitchen, Edward placed bowls on the counter and filled them with Honey Tubes while Nicky tried to read his mother's newspaper.

"Is this right? M.i.s.s.ing…missing…ch.i.l."

Edward swooped over and moved the paper out of his reach.

"Might be better to practise reading with storybooks, some of that stuff can be scary."

Ding dong!

The doorbell chimed and they heard their mother's footsteps hurry down the stairs. After a short, mumbled conversation, the noise of the hoover drifted up from the hall and a few minutes later their mother dashed into the kitchen, her heels click clicking on the tiles. She was like a whirlwind, already dressed for business in a white trouser suit, her immaculate blonde hair bouncing in soft curls around her pretty face.

"Morning, my lovelies," she beamed. "The cleaning lady's here now, she'll be in charge until Claudette gets back from her night off. I'm sorry but I must dash, I love you my darlings, stay out of trouble and I'll see you tomorrow."

She hugged them as best she could, her hands full of her briefcase and overnight bag, before plonking a big pink-lipstick kiss on the top of Nicky's head, and one on Edward's cheek.

"Bye Mummy, we love you too," they chorused back, with mouths full of Honey Tubes.

After she'd gone, both boys wrinkled and wiggled their noses, she'd slightly over perfumed as usual.

Nicky looked at his brother dejectedly.

"I really wanted to ask her today," he sulked. "I've decided I'd like a rainbow coloured one."

Edward laughed while rubbing the sticky, glossy lipstick

from his cheek.

"I know Nicky, but she has to work. Maybe I can send her an email later? There's no need to be sad; remember we're having a picnic for lunch. Let's get changed and go outside."

Nicky, delighted at the prospect of a day spent in the garden, sprang up and cartwheeled towards the kitchen door.

"Race you upstairs, whoever's the slowest at getting dressed can make it," he shouted, knowing full well Edward would let him win.

Within a matter of seconds, both boys were in t-shirts and shorts hurtling back down but as they reached the bottom of the stairs, Edward put out a steadying hand.

"Slow down," he whispered. "Don't forget the cleaning lady's down there, Nicky."

Apprehensively, Nicky's big blue eyes looked up at his brother.

"Don't worry, we'll keep out of her way," Edward smiled.

"But she looks so mean, like the crossest, crabbiest crow I've ever seen and she's always scowling. I bet she'd suck me up in her vacuum cleaner if she could!" Nicky's words tumbled out anxiously.

"She's fine, you're being over-dramatic," Edward replied, patting him reassuringly. "Mummy wouldn't leave us with her if she wasn't okay. Come on, let's try to get past without getting spotted. We can pretend it's a game."

The boys peered around the bottom of the stairs. The backdoor seemed far away with the cleaning lady blocking their path.

Dressed in her usual black housecoat and matching cleaning-lady headscarf, Nicky was right; she was made of nightmares. A shadowy figure ready to make you scream until your hair turned white. Her sharp bony face was covered in wrinkles like a dried-up prune that had sat in the sun for a month and she was always mumbling bad temperedly to herself. The boys watched as her dark beady eyes darted this way and that, scanning for specs of dust, or little boys, to destroy.

But, with no alternative route into the garden, they'd have to sneak past her. They waited patiently until she turned away from them.

"Now's our chance, Nicky. Don't make a sound. I'll go first," whispered Edward.

Tiptoeing through the hall, he made it to the door without being spotted before gesturing for his brother to follow. Nicky took the same route and got within a few yards when suddenly Mrs M spun around.

Somewhat surprised by her swift movement, Nicky fell backwards, landing on her shopping trolley. It wobbled and tipped over, crashing to the ground and a small booklet flew out, sliding across the shiny floor. Nicky grabbed the trolley while Edward hastily retrieved the booklet.

"Sorry," they said nervously.

Mrs M eyeballed the quaking boys.

"Whatever's the matter with you two?" she replied, glowering at them through narrowed eyes.

"Nothing, Mrs M." Edward answered bravely and, taking a quick glance, handed the booklet back.

As they stood in front of her, frozen to the spot, Nicky's nose tingled. A strong smell of furniture polish clawed its way up his nostrils, adding to the tickle of his mother's perfume. Instinctively, he raised his hand to his nose and began poking about.

"Well, I think you'd better do 'nothing' somewhere else!" she snapped.

Then, she turned to Nicky.

"But before you do, I suggest you remove your finger before it gets stuck!"

The little boy quickly obeyed but, on its tip, sat a large sticky lump of snot. He looked about for somewhere to put it but, with nothing to hand, popped it in his mouth.

Mrs M scowled before gesturing with her duster towards the door, indicating that they were free to go. Then she watched as they disappeared into the garden. With the trap set, she allowed a sly smile to inch its way across her face, something she only did when things were going her way.

Chapter Three
Up a Tree

Cucumber climbed to the highest branch of the tallest tree and deliberately started scuffing her shoes. She loved them but the last few days had left her feeling very annoyed so she'd taken her frustration out on the shiny patent leather. Since Cassie's accident, the adults had been behaving strangely secretive and, as yet, The Boss hadn't asked her to take the starring role.

To add to the mystery, when she'd gone in search of breakfast that morning, they'd been busy preparing a feast the likes of which she'd never seen. Plates covered in cling film were piling up filled with triangle-shaped sandwiches, prawn cocktail crisps, cocktail sausages, slices of pepperoni pizza, sweet popcorn, small pink wafers, oblong chocolate biscuits, sugared doughnuts and rainbow coloured cupcakes.

"Who's this for?" Cucumber had asked, reaching up and taking a slice of pepperoni pizza before hiding it in her satchel.

"A special guest, my darling, why don't you play outside, it's a lovely day," was Bernard's reply.

"Why are they coming here?" she'd tried again.

"You'll find out later Cucumber, now run along dear and try not to get under our feet."

They never had guests so, with no other way of finding out what was going on, she climbed up the tree and started spying on them.

Below her stood the old hospital. Once a glorious building, it was now a shadow of its former self. The plaster was cracking and large sections had crumbled off, lying in heaps on the dry earth below. Some windows had complete panes of glass, but the majority held shattered fragments or were covered with ugly sheets of hardboard. The roof had so many missing tiles it looked like a checkerboard and let the rain in but, on the bright side, it provided the perfect nesting place for Bernard's doves.

Behind the main building was a wasteland of grit and stones which had once been a car park. Mrs M's grotty looking caravan sat on its own in the far corner, as far away as possible from the hospital. The Boss had left long before Cucumber had woken, probably to one of her cleaning jobs, and her lair stood silent and empty, its door firmly closed.

To the left were several outbuildings, held together with rusty nails and glue, a forbidden place which Cucumber often snuck into. In the distance, a scruffy hedge bordered an enormous field full of daisies. Harriet, the youngest of the dogs, was playing below her, chasing her tail.

Time ticked by slowly and boredom crept in so Cucumber began plaiting a small section of her hair. It was black and glossy but only reached to her chin so it didn't take long to finish. The little girl glanced down again and was just wondering whether to give up and go inside when Bernard came shuffling into view. Leaning forward, she peered through the leaves as the old man placed a ladder against a tree. Then, climbing to the top, he secured a banner. Another adult appeared. It was Mrs S carrying cups and saucers on her Zimmer frame. Considering she was so ancient and had such a big load, it seemed miraculous that nothing fell.

"You okay with that lot?" Bernard shouted over to her.

"Bernard, you old joker, course I am, years of practise," she chortled, laying the crockery out.

This made Cucumber laugh too until she remembered she was cross.

Eventually, the other residents appeared. Mr F, bandy-legged and supported by a walking stick. He looked about 102 years old. Mr D, dressed in a three-piece suit, complete with an old-fashioned pocket watch on a chain. A slightly younger Mr A, in a t-shirt and shorts and finally, Mrs D, in a bright yellow boiler suit, purchased some thirty years previously.

They began setting out tables and chairs which they covered in bright blue fabric. Another few minutes ticked by without incident until Mr and Mrs G arrived wearing matching tracksuits in a deep shade of purple. Checking his clipboard, Mr G began issuing instructions to his wife who was busy polishing the cutlery.

"Make sure you've got a matching set, don't want the old goat coming home and kicking up a stink," he barked.

"Darling, please try to relax," she replied, "and please don't call Mrs M an old goat!"

"But she is," he said under his breath.

Aunty H, her silver-white hair in rollers and fluffy slippers on her feet, emerged from the old hospital. She was carrying parcels wrapped in blue paper tied with gold ribbon which she placed on the corner of a table.

As they worked, Mr and Mrs G continued to snap at one another. Cucumber had never heard them speak like that and it made her more determined to find out what they were up to.

Once the preparations for the party were complete, the adults huddled together and began talking in hushed tones. Cucumber couldn't hear them so she shuffled forward but as she did, her legs wobbled and her bottom slid off the branch. Her stomach lurched as she grabbed hold of the branch with both arms, hugging it tightly. The adults stopped talking and glanced over to where she clung on but didn't seem to spot her. After a few moments, they returned to their conversation. Cucumber took a deep breath and swung herself back up before clambering to the ground and creeping under one of the covered tables. A few seconds later Harriet, the dog, bounded in and, pleased to see the little girl, started licking her face.

"Shhhh! Stop!" Cucumber soothed whilst scratching the puppy behind the ears. "You've got to be quiet. I need to find out what's going on."

Harriet carried on licking.

"…course, it'll be a success," was the first thing she heard Bernard say. "I know we haven't done it for years but it's in our blood, we were born to it."

"We were," Mr G agreed, "but you've got to admit, changing Cassie's position could be dangerous, don't you think she could still do the routine, she's got a little time to recover?"

"I'm sorry," replied Bernard gravely, "but I don't think her leg can do the jumps and I'm worried her arm won't be strong enough for the bit at the end. Let's be honest, if it goes wrong, it'll be a disaster. I'm sad for the little mite, she's worked so hard but she knows the plan and I've explained she'll be sharing the spotlight. I've told her I'm relying on her to get everyone into position."

"You're right Bernard, at least this way Cassie can still perform," agreed Aunty H.

"Absolutely, besides, I'm sure we've been in worse situations than this, haven't we?" Bernard was trying to sound positive.

Mr G looked at him doubtfully.

"Once Mrs M's back we'll see what she's picked up and then make the final changes, it'll be fine."

The others smiled, trying to catch his enthusiasm.

Bernard glanced at his pocket watch.

"We've got a few hours, let's not waste them worrying. We should put our feet up while we can."

Everyone agreed and Cucumber waited while they drifted back inside the old hospital before crawling from underneath the table. The conversation hadn't told her a great deal, but she knew one thing. Whatever Mrs M was up to, it was important.

Cucumber blinked in the brilliant sunshine as she checked no one was watching. Then she raced across the car park and slipped inside Mrs M's caravan. Once there, she took out her picture diary and carefully copied the words on The Boss's wall planner.

Reaching inside Mrs M's wardrobe, she took out a long, brown checked skirt and a purple shawl.

Chapter Four
Talking Bush

In the middle of the garden, arms held high, Nicky raised one leg and raced forward. Tucking his head in he somersaulted up and over before bouncing back onto the balls of his feet. He focused and then launched into a cartwheel followed by another effortless somersault. Pleased with the routine he pulled his body up straight and grinned, glancing over to where Edward sat in the treehouse.

With Edward's nose deeply engrossed in his magic book, Nicky could only see the top of his head. He wished his brother would look up occasionally and give him feedback or even a little encouragement, but it was pointless. His brother didn't have a clue about gymnastics and besides, he was happy in his own world, working out card tricks or how to saw people in half. Nicky hoped he'd never have to be his assistant!

Ready for the next sequence, he was about to raise his leg when the bush nearest spoke.

"*Pssst!*" it said.

He stared at it for a few moments but it didn't move, didn't make a sound, so he lifted his leg again.

"*Pssst!*" it repeated.

"Ed, the b-b-bush is talking," he stammered.

"That's good, Nicky," replied Edward, not paying attention.

Nicky tried to concentrate, he'd seen a gymnastics programme on the telly about audiences and the ways they could be distracting. Examples had been given of sweet bag rustling or loud coughing but there'd been no mention of talking shrubs. Nicky knew he had to focus so curled into a forward roll before pushing himself off the ground with his hands. His body flew high into the sky as he flipped over and landed back on his feet facing the bush. In front of him stood a girl.

She was older and taller than him, possibly Edward's age or even as old as a teenager. Nicky thought she had a wise face. He liked her eyes, deep brown, huge, kind and confident.

"Hello," she whispered. "You're fantastic, aren't you?"

"Th-th-thank you," he whispered back.

"Would you like a sweet?" she asked, offering him the bag.

"Th-th-thank you," he whispered again, helping himself to a strawberry shoelace.

"We have them all the time back at camp," said the girl. "It's part of the training regime, keeps our energy up."

"Training regime?" Nicky looked quizzically at her while chewing.

"Yes, oh sorry, I forgot to introduce myself. I'm Cassie, from the Gymnastics Training Programme, pleased to meet you," she extended her hand.

Nicky shook it, he'd never heard of the Gymnastics Training Programme but it sounded grand.

"I'm a talent spotter, we travel the country spotting talent."

Then, she produced a clipboard from behind her back

and began studying it.

"I've been making notes and I think with a little work you might be suitable."

Nicky couldn't believe his ears.

"Me? Are you joking? That's wonderful!" His response was enthusiastic.

"Steady on," replied Cassie, trying to calm the little boy. "You have to pass the exam first!"

"Will I?" Nicky waited patiently for further explanation.

"Yes, but there's something I need to tell you." Cassie leant in, millimetres from his nose. "The Gymnastics Programme is a secret, a BIG secret."

Then she glanced secretively left and right before fixing her eyes on his.

"Other countries are desperate to know about the programme, so we need to make sure we can trust you." Again, she checked before continuing. "First, you need to come to the camp and then, if you pass the exam, we'll let your family know and you can join the team."

"When can I come to the camp?" he asked.

"Today, but…" she paused again, purposefully glancing towards the top of Edward's head. "If he discovers you've gone, before we know it, 'nee nah, nee nah', he'll call the police and the secret will be out."

Nicky looked at her earnestly.

"Don't worry, Mummy's away and our au pair doesn't pay any attention when she's watching telly," his eyebrows knitted, a look of concentration on his face as he considered his escape. "I'll tell Edward I'm doing my homework and mustn't be disturbed."

Instantly he knew, by the look on her face, he'd have to come up with a better plan.

He thought again. "I could tell him I've got a business meeting?"

Cassie raised her eyebrows, suppressing a giggle.

"No, you're right, that's even sillier, I don't have a job."

Nicky glanced towards the treehouse, waiting for a lightbulb moment. There was no way he was going to let an opportunity like this slip through his fingers.

Eventually, *PING*, it came to him.

"Wait there, I won't be long," he said, before somersaulting across the garden, into the house.

By the time he returned Cassie had settled back in the bush with a large toffee. He waited while she crawled out and then placed a postcard at the bottom of the treehouse ladder.

"Can I have another sweet please?" Nicky asked.

"Sure!" she said, holding out the bag.

Wafts of caramel, liquorice, bonbons and sherbet filled his nostrils, it was a difficult decision but finally, he selected a big juicy toffee and popped it on top of the postcard.

"But how can I get out of here without being caught?" Nicky scratched his head.

"You'll see!" replied Cassie mysteriously and began walking towards the back door.

Nicky followed eagerly, oblivious to one small detail. The Gymnastics Training Programme didn't exist!

Chapter Five
Barking Up the Wrong Tree

Cucumber sighed with relief when she finally made it to the bus stop without either tripping or walking into a lamp post. Mrs M's borrowed skirt was far too long, and the shawl kept falling over her face, making the journey hazardous.

Once there, she briefly considered changing back into her normal clothes but after catching her reflection in the glass of shelter, decided against it. It was the perfect disguise, and she chuckled as she congratulated herself, certain no one would recognise her dressed as a little old lady going about her little old lady business.

As the bus pulled up, the driver greeted her cheerily, "Hey Cucumber, where are you off to?"

"How did you know it was me?" she replied disappointedly.

"Your bag," the driver pointed at the big yellow 'C' stitched on the satchel. "You always have it with you."

"Oh," she turned it over quickly, hiding the letter.

"And now?" she asked hopefully.

"Sorry," the driver laughed. "Never seen you before, where are you going, Madam?"

Cucumber giggled.

"Here!" she said, holding out her picture diary with the scribbled address.

The driver examined it.

"Yes, Madam, Apple Blossom Crescent's on my route, sit behind and I'll let you know when we get there."

"Thank you," replied Cucumber, but she'd only taken a few steps when the driver called her back.

"Aren't you forgetting someone?"

Cucumber followed her gaze to where Harriet sat on the pavement, wagging her tail.

"Oh Harriet, you shouldn't have followed me!" she

scolded, picking the puppy up.

With her arms full, she stuffed the ticket in her pocket before clambering onto the seat immediately behind the driver. Her feet didn't touch the ground, so she held on tightly, one hand on Harriet, the other gripping the seat and tried to remember the conversation she'd overheard between the adults. They were expecting Mrs M to pick something up and, as the bus trundled up Station Road, Cucumber tried to guess what it might be. It wasn't long before she'd run out of ideas.

That was until a bright yellow dress, hanging in a shop window, caught her attention and a small worm of an idea began burrowing up through the earth in her brain. Cassie's costume wouldn't fit her and Bernard, who usually made them, wouldn't have had time to rustle one up. What if Mrs M had gone in search of a new costume?

As she thought about the adults' odd behaviour, their secretiveness and unwillingness to involve her in the party preparations, her mind soon raced to a very unlikely conclusion. They'd mentioned some changes, Cassie having to share the spotlight, it could only mean one thing, the party was for her! She bounced up and down imagining the moment they'd present her with the new costume and ask her to step in. Everyone would cheer and she'd dance and it would be the best day ever…

"Madam," the driver called again and then, "Cucumber."

"Huh?" replied the little girl, remembering where she was.

"This is Apple Blossom Crescent. Do you know which way to go?"

"I think so," she replied, sounding slightly confused.

"Number 8's on the left, lovey."

Cucumber thanked the driver and watched as the bus disappeared over the brow of the hill before turning her attention towards Apple Blossom Crescent.

A familiar figure emerged from a house and began striding towards her, sending her into a panic. Frantically, she dashed this way and that, trying to hide, but the skirt kept tripping her and it was only at the last minute she spotted a bush and dived in, Harriet landing on her with a thud.

Luckily Mrs M hadn't noticed. Her shopping trolley had caught on some paving stones and Cucumber giggled as she heaved the enormous bag backwards and forwards, trying to drag it free. A few minutes into the struggle, a funny-looking couple emerged from a house and began arguing loudly. Mrs M stopped instantly and pretended to fiddle with her cleaning lady's headscarf until they'd driven away and then started talking to the bag. Cucumber couldn't hear what she was saying, but it tipped forward on its own and The Boss continued her journey. Finally, she disappeared around the corner at the bottom of the road, as though nothing had happened.

Cucumber, stunned, and more than a little confused by what she'd witnessed, was keen to record it in her picture diary.

Every day she pasted images from newspapers and magazines and drew pictures in it, recording the day's events. Mostly, nothing of much interest happened, so she allowed herself a bit of creativity, the odd dragon or football player. It brightened the pages and made life a little more fun. Today was different though, there was a lot going on and she couldn't wait to get started.

Taking the diary and a magazine from her satchel, she began leafing through them while keeping an eye on Number 8, Apple Blossom Crescent.

It was one of the biggest houses she'd ever seen and she noticed, with a hint of jealousy, the spectacular treehouse in the garden. She could see the top of a brown-haired head and made a mental note to add it to her picture later.

With Harriet happily dozing by her side, she turned to

the page in her diary where she'd drawn Cassie's routine. She added a cheese sandwich, cut from a magazine, and it made her giggle as she remembered Mrs M crashing to the ground and Bernard flapping about like an old dodo.

After a while Harriet began to stretch, yawn and sniff. She could smell the pepperoni pizza in Cucumber's satchel so the little girl took out the slice and shared it with the puppy. Then she started searching the magazine for an image of a dress similar to the one she'd seen in the shop. Eventually, she found what she was after and had just started cutting it out when she remembered the bus. Not wanting to miss it, but keen to get a closer look at Number 8, she started packing her diary, scissors and glue away.

Chapter Six
The Disappearance

Time whizzed by and Edward hadn't realised how late it was when he finally emerged from the depths of his magic book. He'd been enjoying it so much that only the sound of his tummy and the nagging pain inside made him stop reading.

He'd been studying the book for months in the hope he'd learn enough to become a professional magician. So far, he'd taught himself two rope tricks, three card tricks and one with balls and a cup.

A magician who used doves had written the book. Soft

and silent they flew across the stage until **'BAM'**, he made them disappear in a great big puff of smoke. Edward fancied having a go himself and for several weeks had been feeding the birds in the garden. Fat pigeons had been the most interested, but Edward wasn't sure they'd be right for his act. They crashed out of the sky, landing with a heavy **'DOFF'** when they hit the ground, not at all as graceful as a dove!

His tummy rumbled and Edward realised it was way past lunchtime. Much earlier he'd heard Mr and Mrs Groucher from Number 16 arguing as they'd set off in their car. They were an odd-looking couple; she towering over him like an enormous bison wearing a flowery dress and a wig of great big orange curls. While Mr Groucher reminded Edward of a hyena. Stringy, furtive and greying around the edges.

They'd already driven off when he'd glanced up but he'd spotted Mrs M disappearing around the corner at the bottom of the road, dragging her shopping trolley behind her.

Now, as he stood at the top of the ladder, it was much quieter. The fluffy tortoiseshell cat that lived at Number 13 lay on the warm tarmacked road basking in the sunshine. A squirrel hopped along the ground. A fat pigeon crash-landed on the pavement, and a puppy raced from a bush. Edward chuckled as it chased the tortoiseshell cat up a tree and a little old lady stumbled from the bush after it. She looked like she was trying to catch a bar of soap in the bath.

At the bottom of the ladder, Edward saw a postcard lying on the ground. He recognised his brother's writing straight away but couldn't make out the words. On top, Nicky had left a sweet wrapped in gold foil and cellophane. Edward held it to his nose and inhaled deeply, it didn't smell like a normal toffee; it was lemonier, with a hint of floor polish.

"Odd?!" said Edward out loud, but he was hungry and eagerly unwrapped it before popping it in his mouth.

Closing his eyes for a few moments he savoured the flavour, it really was scrummy, creamy and not lemony at all. Eventually, he opened his eyes again and found the bush-dwelling old lady standing next to him. At her feet sat the puppy, enthusiastically licking the postcard.

"No!" Edward cried.

Desperately he tried to retrieve the postcard from the puppy's slobbering tongue but it was too late, the words were all smudged.

"Oh dear," whispered the old lady. "Was it important?"

"I don't know," replied Edward. "I didn't have time to

read it. It was from my brother."

"Oh well, why don't you ask him?"

Her head tilted upwards but he couldn't see her face inside the heavy shawl.

"I don't know where he is," he replied, distracted by his brother's disappearance.

"Well, you know what little kids are like, they're always escaping," she giggled girlishly. "I'm sure nothing bad has happened… anyway, I want to know if there's a place to buy a costume around here?"

"What?" he replied, confused by the question.

"I thought you might know where to get one, does your mother sew?"

The old lady waited for an answer, but Edward was already walking away.

Then, remembering his manners, he turned.

"I'm sorry but you must excuse me. I need to find my brother, he's only small and Mum likes me to keep an eye on him."

"While she's making costumes?" Edward didn't reply, so she tried again. "I'm sorry but I really must know. I have a bus to catch."

Edward glanced at the top of the hill.

"You mean that one?" he said, pointing at the bus

making its way slowly back towards Apple Blossom Crescent.

The little old lady let out a tiny shriek before dashing across the garden, the puppy scampering behind.

"You didn't tell me your name," Edward called after her.

The little old lady spun round.

"Oh, it's Cuc..." she hesitated while scanning the garden, her eyes coming to rest on the vegetable patch. "I mean Cabbage, yes that's it, Mrs Cabbage."

"My mum doesn't sew, Mrs Cabbage," Edward yelled.

"Blast!" she replied.

As she reached the gate, Edward noticed a tiny piece of paper flutter from her pocket. He called out, but it was too late, she'd already gone.

Back inside the house, Edward told Claudette that he and Nicky were playing hide and seek. Then he worked meticulously through each room checking and re-checking but by the time he'd reached the last one, he had to admit his brother had disappeared, completely and utterly.

Chapter Seven
The Party

Mrs M's journey back to the old hospital took several hours. The weight of the children inside the trolley meant she couldn't get on the bus without raising suspicion so she had to walk all the way. But it didn't bother her and she strutted up Station Road like a determined flamingo.

Nicky was amazed how clean the inside of a vacuum cleaner bag was and to begin with, he sat quietly. However, with every jolt of the trolley, Cassie's elbows dug into his ribs, making him wince. To distract himself, he started nervously asking questions.

"W-w-where a-a-are w-w-we?" he stammered.

"Where? Where do you think we are?" Cassie laughed.

"W-w-we're inside the v-v-vacuum c-c-cleaner, I c-can't b-b-believe it! H-h-how?" Nicky spluttered.

"Bernard invented it, you'll meet him soon, it's the best feeling ever isn't it, being sucked up by the vacuum? Now stop wiggling, we'll get back faster if you relax."

Nicky tried, but excitement continued to bubble up inside him.

"Will all the gymnasts be there?" he whispered.

"Sort of," Cassie replied mysteriously. "Now *sssshhhh*!"

As the journey continued, Nicky listened to the rumble of the street outside. Engines revved, cars beeped and occasionally he could hear people chattering. Eventually, it grew quieter, and they stopped.

"Where are we?" Nicky asked for the second time.

"Home!" shouted Cassie, unzipping the bag and jumping out. "Come on, Nicky, everyone's waiting!"

Once alone, Nicky felt anxious. His tummy growled, and he began to think about the picnic Edward had promised him. Breakfast had been a long time ago. Nervously he picked his nose whilst wondering whether his brother had found the postcard and a twinge of worry and another rumble made his tummy twist.

Cassie's head shot back in.

"What's the matter, Nicky?" she asked kindly. "Everyone excited to meet you, they've made tea, and the band's ready to play."

Nicky held her hand tightly as he crawled into the daylight and slowly rose to his feet. Blinking in the afternoon sunshine he gazed left and right and then back again. In front of him stood a line of old people, their beaming faces putting him at ease. Behind, balloons and streamers hung in the trees, framing a large blue banner. It said, 'Welcome Nicky'.

"Wow!" he exclaimed. "Is this for me?"

One of the old people stepped forward, a gentleman with great, big, grey, bushy eyebrows and twinkly eyes. Immaculately dressed, he wore clean, pressed trousers and a woollen tank top. He smelt of shaving foam and he'd combed his shiny, grey hair straight back over the top of his head.

"Hello Nicky, I'm Bernard. Thank you for coming to see us. Can I get you some food?"

"Oh yes please, Bernard. I'm starving."

Nicky's tummy rumbled again as Bernard crammed his plate with treats and handed it to him. He took a bite out of a doughnut covered with chocolate icing and tried not to stare as Mrs M packed the vacuum cleaner back inside the shopping trolley.

"Don't feed him too much, Bernard. He needs to stay light on his feet," she snapped.

Bernard winked at the little boy and eased himself into a battered old armchair, patting a small deckchair next to him.

"Come and take a seat young man, we've got a lot to talk about," he said warmly.

The band began to play. Mr A, on guitar, twanged while Mrs D, on saxophone, swung. Mr G kept time, drumming out a jaunty pace. Nicky couldn't help but tap his feet in time to the music.

"What do you think?" asked Bernard.

"I think it's wonderful," Nicky replied, a great, big cheesy grin on his face.

As the party continued, Nicky told Bernard about his family. It made him happy to think of them, but also a little homesick. All the time he wondered when he'd hear about the training programme and, more excitingly, when he'd do the exam Cassie had mentioned.

With dusk settling, Aunty H approached, her arms full of presents.

"We've got a few bits and bobs for you, to make you feel at home. You'll need them later so why not open them before it gets too dark?"

Inside the first parcel was a set of pyjamas which he rubbed against his cheek, they were fluffy, the fluffiest he'd ever felt and they smelt of lavender.

"Thank you, Aunty H."

"Aren't you a polite boy?" she said, smiling delightedly at him.

Then she turned to Mrs M. "Doesn't he have lovely manners?"

The Boss fixed him with a piercing stare.

"Manners are not important, he just needs to make sure he does what he's told," and with that, she stalked off to her caravan.

Aunty H rolled her eyes and grinned.

"Ignore her. She can seem a bit grumpy at times."

The next present was a flannel with small golden stars and his name embroidered across the middle in large looping letters. A toothbrush came after in the same shade of blue, at the end an 'N' in gold. Finally, a golden torch covered in small sparkling stones which glittered, it was the most beautiful torch he'd ever seen.

"Thank you very much," he said, wondering why he'd

need it all.

"You're welcome, they'll come in handy."

"When can I do the examination?" he couldn't wait any longer.

"Well, the thing is Nicky, I have something to confess. This might come as a bit of a shock, but we haven't been entirely honest with you." Bernard had a grave look on his face. "You see there is no Gymnastics Training Programme."

Nicky's mind raced, no gymnastics, no training programme?

Reading his thoughts, Bernard continued.

"I think it's time to show you, it's the easiest way to explain, come with me young man," and taking hold of Nicky's hand he led him towards a gap in the hedge.

Behind sat an enormous field circled by trees. In the middle, burning fiercely, was a huge bonfire and in the far corner a large white van which had seen better days. Nicky wondered why he hadn't smelt the woody smoke of the fire before but in some ways, was glad he hadn't. The whole thing felt sinister and then, to add to his worry, a figure appeared out of the darkness.

Mrs M, dressed completely in black, positioned herself in front of the fire. Nicky could see the outline of her body as the flames leapt and crackled and, despite the heat, a chill ran through his bones.

She was menacing, her face set in a haughty sneer, lip curling on one side. One eyebrow lifted as she glared down the bridge of her nose and her eyes glittered wickedly. He looked for Cassie, for some kind of reassurance but realised, with horror, he hadn't seen her since their arrival.

Bernard nudged him and nodded towards Mrs M. The little boy dragged his attention back to her, he'd never been comfortable around the old lady. Recently he'd caught her staring at him, a look of disgust on her face, and now it dawned on him how much she reminded him of a storybook villain. The type who stole children and cooked them.

Nicky gulped as once more his tummy began to twist and turn. Frantically he cast an eye about, wondering whether he should make a run for it.

Chapter Eight

Edward the Magician

For a few seconds, Edward thought about telling Claudette he'd lost his brother and then immediately changed his mind. Nicky had left a note which probably meant he was already making his way back to Apple Blossom Crescent. It seemed silly getting into trouble and worrying everyone unnecessarily.

Returning to the treehouse, Edward settled back to wait for his brother but, leafing through the pages of his magic book, chapter after chapter passed in front of his eyes and he couldn't remember a single word. Every few minutes he looked up, expecting to see Nicky walk through the gate but as the sun set, hope was fading.

Edward's eyes grew tired and began to get sore from reading and watching so, reluctantly, he packed his books away.

Back inside Number 8, he could smell the spikey chemical perfume of nail varnish. With one eye on the telly and the other on her hand, Edward could see Claudette busy with film stars and a dazzling shade of orange. As he walked past, in the most unsuspicious way he could manage, he began talking.

"Nicky's going to bed now," he said.

"Hmmm," she replied.

He got to the stairs.

"I'll tuck him up and then maybe read for a bit if that's okay?"

"Hmmm," she replied again, still not dragging her eyes from the telly.

"See you in the morning," he said in his normal voice and then, "night, night" in a slightly higher one, trying to imitate his little brother.

"Good night, Edward. Good night, Nicky." She still hadn't taken her eyes from the box.

Phew! Edward thought.

In his bedroom, he scanned his bookcase, wondering which of his treasures would help him find his brother. Halfway through the first shelf, he spotted *Disappearing and Vanishing Tricks: Volume One* and began leafing through the pages. He assumed if he found out how to make someone disappear it would be easy to make them reappear. Edward searched for loud bangs and puffs of smoke and in a rush to get to the real magic, started turning the pages quickly. But, by the end, he realised he'd been stupid. Nicky hadn't disappeared because of a trick and it was foolish to imagine he could simply magic his brother back.

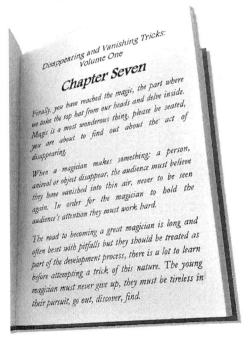

Disappearing and Vanishing Tricks: Volume One

Chapter Seven

Finally, you have reached the magic, the part where we take the top hat from our heads and delve inside. Magic is a most wonderous thing, please be seated, you are about to find out about the act of disappearing.

When a magician makes something; a person, animal or object disappear, the audience must believe they have vanished into thin air, never to be seen again. In order for the magician to hold the audience's attention they must work hard.

The road to becoming a great magician is long and often beset with pitfalls but they should be treated as part of the development process, there is a lot to learn before attempting a trick of this nature. The young magician must never give up, they must be tireless in their pursuit, go out, discover, find.

His only clue had been the postcard, but the slobbering puppy had destroyed it and it left him with nothing. Tears began forming in the corner of his eyes and a feeling of sick hopelessness swept over him. Raising a hand to wipe them away, he noticed a toffee wrapper stuck to his sleeve. It was the one his brother had left and as he peeled it off, smoothing the shiny plastic, he saw gold letters printed on the cellophane.

The letters were familiar, he'd seen them before but, try as he might, couldn't remember where. Edward glanced at the book again, the last few words coming into sharp focus.

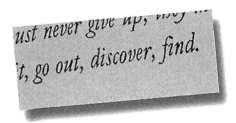

ust never give up, they ...
t, go out, discover, find.

Edward was pleased, magic had helped! Although he would not find his brother in the pages of a book, it had told him what to do!

He imagined searching for his brother dressed in a long black cloak and top hat, the style of stage costume he wanted when he was a famous magician. It was old-fashioned but all his heroes wore it, the ones in the grainy black and white pictures. The only problem, he'd probably look ridiculous.

No, he needed something that would allow him to blend into his surroundings. That way, if he bumped into someone he knew, which was likely, they wouldn't recognise him and start asking awkward questions, like where his brother was.

With nothing suitable in his wardrobe, Edward decided he'd have to borrow something from his mother's costume drawer. She loved a fancy-dress party and had a wide selection of outfits.

Slipping across the landing into her room he inhaled

deeply. It smelled of her perfume, the one she wore when they'd said goodbye that morning. The familiar aroma comforted him so he tiptoed over to her dressing table and picked up the perfume bottle before blasting a few sprays into the air.

It made his nose tickle.

Actually, it was more than a tickle. It was a great big tingle, itching its way up his nostrils.

Oh, no!

The sneeze was making its way back down his nose!

If Claudette heard, she'd want to know what he was up to or worse still, where Nicky was.

Quickly he raced across to his mother's bed and dived under the covers.

Aaaaccccchhhooooo!

It was the second loudest sneeze he'd ever done and instantly reminded him of the loudest and most embarrassing one of his life.

It had happened in assembly just as the Head Teacher was talking about not setting off fire alarms (or something equally boring).

His nose had tingled all morning but the sneeze, when

it came, had caught him by surprise. It blasted out without warning, the noise shooting through the teachers who were gently snoozing on the stage.

Mrs Peaman, the chemistry teacher, was the first to react. She leapt into the air but as she did, her chair crashed backwards taking Mr Barnacle's from underneath him. She tried valiantly to save him but it didn't work.

CRASH!

She smashed straight into Mrs Flowers, the PE teacher.

Mrs Flowers and her chair both skidded off the stage while Mrs Peaman carried on, rocketing straight into the Head Teacher who then dominoed into the Deputy Head.

The hall erupted into fits of giggles while Edward turned to his best friend Gary and asked whether he should help untangle the tangle of teachers. Luckily, between the tears and hiccups of laughter, Gary told him to laugh.

To begin with, Edward hadn't understood but took the advice and it was only afterwards he realised how his friend had saved him. With a sea of giggling children rolling around in front of them, the teachers had found it impossible to locate the guilty party and assembly had ended. Edward was grateful; his best friend had rescued him from a lifetime of detentions.

While shuddering at the memory, he straightened the

bedclothes and padded across to the chest of drawers containing his mother's fancy dress costumes.

Rummaging through, he selected a few items and then slipped across the landing to his brother's room. It still amazed him that Nicky hadn't bothered to take anything, not even clean underwear! He needed to help him cover his tracks so, to fool Claudette, he stuffed a pillow under the duvet. Next, he grabbed a couple of pairs of clean pants and popped them at the bottom of his rucksack.

Back in his own room, he added a magic book, a notepad, a pen, a torch, and his wallet. It only contained five pounds but, reluctant to raid his money box (he'd been saving for a new trick), it would have to do. Then he tucked himself into bed and began examining the soggy postcard and sweet wrapper, trying to decide where to start his search. He was positive he was missing something but, try as he might, couldn't think what.

Chapter Nine
The Truth?

Cucumber's bus journey home had been miserable, the trip was a complete waste of time. There'd been no costume, and she felt silly for getting so fantastically carried away.

Jumping from the bus with Harriet by her side, she was about to sneak through the gates of the old hospital when she heard the band playing, the party in full swing.

The little girl was not in the mood and didn't want to get caught dressed in Mrs M's borrowed clothes so she crossed the road and slipped into the library garden.

After changing, she sat on a bench and ripped out the image of the new costume she'd stuck in her picture diary only hours before. Tearing it into pieces she tried desperately to stop the flow of hot, angry tears that threatened to fall.

She didn't succeed, and it was only when the light began to fade that the crying stopped and she went home.

Luckily, she arrived just in time.

"Where have you been?" Cassie asked irritably. "I've been looking for you for ages."

"Why?" she replied, trying to look innocent. "I fell asleep in a tree is all!"

Cassie looked the little girl up and down suspiciously. She could see the little girl's eyes were red and puffy and knew she'd been up to something.

"Just get changed, you're needed in the field, everyone's waiting!" Cassie snapped, before stalking out of the dormitory.

Cucumber didn't enjoy being bossed around but knew she was already in trouble so grabbed her boiler suit and headed for the bathroom.

Nicky stood next to Bernard, his heart fluttering as Mrs M raised both arms and dropped them swiftly and dramatically. At her signal, Mr A and Mr G rushed forwards, opening the doors of the white van.

Plumes of smoke billowed out, filling the air with the smell of engine oil and petrol. Shuffling backwards, Nicky tried to move away but the steadying hand of Bernard forced him to take a few faltering steps towards the bonfire.

"Look over there, young man."

Bernard pointed at the van as the first motorbike came flying out, closely followed by one, two, three, four, five, six, seven, eight, nine more. Weaving around in intricate patterns, Nicky was astonished as they came within a hair's breadth of crashing.

The riders wore boiler suits, each a different bold, bright colour, and heavy protective gloves. On their feet were sturdy black boots with yellow flamed fins which sparkled like their shiny helmets as they swooped past the flames of the bonfire.

With ease, they slipped past one another like a snake twisting through its own body before leaping and flying like dolphins playing in the ocean. Mesmerised, Nicky tried not to blink.

Finally, they split into two groups which headed to

opposite sides where ramps had been set up in front of the burning pile. Still transfixed, Nicky watched as the first rider screeched off from the left at exactly the same time as another from the right. Hurtling towards the fire, they mounted the ramps and shot upwards.

They were going to crash!

"No!" Nicky shouted as a rider spun their bike and flipped over the top of the other in an arc.

Nicky's mouth dropped open as the other riders followed, cartwheeling and somersaulting over the flames. He'd never seen anything like it, but that's because he'd never seen motorbike gymnastics!

"Are you okay, Nicky?" Bernard asked after the display had finished.

"Wonderful," Nicky finally remembered to breathe. "Did that just happen?"

"It did," chuckled Bernard.

Nicky waited while the bikes roared across the field to where Aunty H was waiting.

"Park up first my darlings," she shouted over the roar of their engines. "Then help yourselves to a little supper but don't take too much, you've already eaten, and it's getting late."

One rider screeched off, swooping around the field

before skidding in front of him. Once they'd flipped their visor up, Nicky recognised the face grinning at him.

"Cassie!"

"Told you it was better than gymnastics," she beamed.

"W-w-was that y-y-you?" he stammered.

"Who did you think it was?" she replied while propping the bike on its stand.

By now the other riders had arrived on foot, they were smiling too.

"Please allow me to introduce you to the Flaming Cycles!" Cassie raised her arm and the Flaming Cycles bowed. "Colin, Collette, Cuthbert, Chloe, Christopher, Charlotte, Craig, Caitlin and Cucumber."

Nicky was awestruck and started gibbering away. "That was amazing, splendid. I've never seen anything like it in my life, never, I'm…I don't know what I am!"

Colin, the eldest, laughed. "Thank you, that's just a warm-up."

Nicky grinned at Colin. He reminded him of Edward with his dark hair falling across his eyes in a sticky, sweaty mess.

"Have you met Harriet?" Colin asked, bending to tickle the puppy playing at his feet.

"No, but I love dogs, she's lovely." Nicky bent to stroke

her.

"She is," Colin grinned. "But not as lovely as food, I'm starving, shall we get some?"

Nicky wasn't the slightest bit hungry but followed Colin back through the hedge with Harriet chasing after them. The Flaming Cycles tucked into the treats while Harriet found a stick and played with Nicky. For a moment he forgot where he was but then the smallest of the Flaming Cycles, dressed in yellow, approached.

"Well, well, well," said Cucumber, her arms folded. "What have we here?"

She looked grumpy.

"Hello," he smiled nervously. "I'm Nicky."

Cucumber turned her head to one side, her feline eyes studying him closely.

"And what are you doing here, Nicky?" she sounded spikey.

Nicky thought for a moment. He knew there was no gymnastics training programme and that meant no exam, he wasn't entirely sure of the answer.

"Um, I don't know," he replied honestly. "Cassie and Mrs M brought me here, they said there was a gymnastic training programme but obviously that's not true."

Cucumber's stare was icy.

"I guess you're good at gymnastics then?" she asked, despite being sure she knew the answer.

"Well, I, I don't know. I practise a lot and it's what I want to be when I grow up."

Cucumber continued to stare.

"Do you know why I'm here?" Nicky asked.

Cucumber's eyes blazed.

"Yes, I think so."

Awkwardly, Nicky waited for her to explain but instead, she flashed him an insincere smile.

"Well, I'm sure they'll tell you soon but, in the meantime, I guess I'd better welcome you to the family. You know it's not that bad living here. Well, not that bad." Cucumber chuckled.

"Welcome me to the family? Live here?"

"Yes!" she replied incredulously. "This is your new home. Didn't they tell you?"

"I can't live here! I already have a family and a home! My Mummy and Edward will miss me." Nicky sounded upset.

Cucumber was astonished.

"I'm sure Cassie told you we're a secret?"

"She did," he had to admit, "but she told me to make an excuse, so my brother wouldn't worry and call the police.

I left him a note, so he wouldn't, but he'll be expecting me back."

Fear flashed across Cucumber's face as she remembered the postcard Harriet had destroyed.

"I hope he doesn't call the police!" she gasped in terror.

"Why?" Nicky asked.

"Because… because," she looked around desperately, "because it would be the worst thing ever!"

Nicky didn't understand. She was scaring him.

"What's going on?" he asked.

Cucumber glanced behind him.

"*Ssshh!* Aunty H's coming over, don't say a word!"

"Well, my little treacle pudding." Aunty H placed an arm around Nicky. "Now you've met the fabulous Flaming Cycles it's time to settle down for the night. You've got a busy day tomorrow."

Chapter Ten

Discovery

Edward woke with a start. He'd dreamt he was in the garden, searching for clues and instantly knew where to go. It was late and his heart pounded with excitement as he crept onto the landing and began padding through the house.

At first, it was strange without the blaring sound of the television and the colours were unfamiliar. Not the usual soft greens and pinks but as though someone had painted everything grey and blue. He briefly wondered whether to rush back upstairs and hide under the covers, but he had to find his brother and needed to be brave.

In the kitchen, he grabbed a packet of biscuits and, ambling over to the fruit bowl, picked out a shiny green apple. His mother's newspaper lay on the counter, the headline illuminated by the silvery moonlight streaming through the window. Until then he'd completely forgotten about it but the memory sent terror zigzagging through his body.

Missing Child!

It has been more than two months since the manager of a home for unwanted children in Bradley Road, Surrey reported the mysterious case of a missing child.

Georgia May George, a tiny orphaned tot, aged 6, vanished along with her pencil case and satchel from the orphanage where she had been living.

The staff had not noticed for a number of weeks. Mr Jefferies, the Manager, stated in an interview that she was a, "very quiet little girl, who often hid and spied on us. I can't really be blamed for not noticing she'd gone."

Mr Jefferies, Bradley Road, Surrey

The police agreed that no one would have noticed and confirmed they are following up on a number of lines of enquiry but believe it likely she has run away. "We are following up on a number of lines of enquiry," said a spokesperson on behalf of the police, stating,

"We believe she is likely to have run away to join the circus or the merchant navy."

A postcard, which appears to be in her handwriting, was left on her bed, it said, 'Gon away, bak at som point, don't wory abowt me.'

Georgia May George is described as being small with chin length black hair. The police have asked anyone who spots a small child, wandering about on their own, to contact them immediately.

Witnesses confirmed there had been a

A creak from upstairs pulled him to his senses so he quickly shoved the newspaper into his rucksack and crept outside.

In the garden, the light of the moon bathed the lawn, but its silver-grey glow didn't reach under the bushes. So, taking his torch out, he lay on the grass and turned its beam on for a few seconds, careful not to alert the neighbours to his midnight adventure.

It wasn't until five bushes into the search that he found what he was after and, reaching in, grabbed the sweet wrapper. He held it to his nose, it had the same unmistakable aroma of lemons and furniture polish like the one his brother had left.

One last sweep of the garden and he was satisfied he'd done a good job. Returning to the house he was about to step inside when he remembered the piece of paper that had fallen out of Mrs Cabbage's pocket. He squinted towards the gate and was pleased to see it still sitting on the grass.

Then…

"NEE NAH! NEE NAH!"

Edward froze.

Blue lights flashed, and the siren cut out.

Racing over to the fence, he peered through a gap,

gasping as a police car pulled onto the driveway and an officer stepped out.

"All looks fine," the officer reported into her radio.

"Okay," came the static-filled reply over the airwaves. "To be honest, the couple who reported it were arguing so loudly I couldn't really hear. Have a quick look and return to base."

"Roger," replied the officer.

"My name's not Roger," came the crackled response.

Edward continued peeking through the fence, watching as the officer scanned the front of the house before returning to her car. Edward thought he was in the clear until, out of the corner of his eye, he spotted a figure dashing across Apple Blossom Crescent. With his dressing-gown flapping and hairy legs glowing white in the dark, Mr Groucher was frantically waving, trying to get the officer's attention.

"Hello, Officer!" Mr Groucher's voice rang out in a shout whisper. "Sorry to bother you, but it was I who made the call."

He paused, waiting for her to congratulate him for his heroism.

"Good Evening, Mr Groucher," she replied politely. "Would you kindly explain what you reported?"

"Yes, I will! There were lights, like a burglar," he confirmed.

The officer took a small notepad from her pocket and began making notes.

"And how would you describe these burglar lights?" asked the officer.

Mr Groucher took a deep breath.

"Flashy, like UFOs," he replied, a smug grin plastered over his face.

"Flashy, like UFO," repeated the officer, writing in her pocketbook.

"Yes, probably about three or four," he added.

"Three or four UFOs," the police officer continued making notes.

Mr Groucher began to redden and his smile slipped from his face.

"I don't mean real UFOs, it's just that's what they reminded me of. It was my wife who thought it might be a burglar."

"Okay, so we're trying to find a burglar or a not real UFO," the police officer replied, trying not to laugh.

"Precisely," nodded Mr Groucher.

"Right," said the officer, zipping the pocketbook back inside her vest. "Let's have a look, shall we? Follow me."

"Follow you?" repeated Mr Groucher. "I'm sorry but I don't think I can…"

Edward snatched the scrap of paper from the grass, he'd heard enough and needed to cover his tracks. Sprinting across the garden, he threw his torch into a bush and then bounded up the treehouse ladder. Leaping inside, he grabbed the spare torch that he kept for emergencies and switched it on as he slid back down the ladder. Once on the ground, he sped towards the back door, hurling the last of the torches into a plant pot before slipping inside the house.

Claudette thundered down the stairs as the police officer and Mr Groucher came striding into view.

"What's going on Edward?" she cried, her hair standing on end as she pulled herself from sleep.

"I don't know Claudette. I came down when I heard the police car. Mr Groucher and the police officer are talking in the garden."

"Wait there!" she commanded, striding towards the door.

Edward was astonished, he'd never seen her move so fast and watched with interest as she flung herself across the lawn. He couldn't hear what she was saying but her voice was louder than normal and at one point she started wagging her finger at Mr Groucher. After that, he scuttled off and the police officer and Claudette headed towards the back door.

Quickly, Edward grabbed his rucksack, chucking it up the stairs just as they came through the door.

"Edward, this is PC O'Brien, she'd like a word with you." Claudette looked serious.

Edward gulped. "Have I done something wrong?" he asked, trying to appear innocent.

"Not really," PC O'Brien replied kindly, "it just might be an idea to switch your torches off when you've been playing with them. Your neighbours, Mr and Mrs Groucher, thought aliens had landed!" she stifled a giggle.

"Oh dear, I am sorry," he blushed. "My brother, Nicky, and I were using them earlier. We must have forgotten about them."

The officer smiled.

"Never mind, no harm done," she said. "My job isn't all about car chases and arresting people."

"But a lot of it is?" Edward asked.

"Every day is different but yes, I have arrested a few people and been in car chases," she nodded.

"That must be exciting," he said, trying to encourage her to keep talking. "Tell me, have you ever found a missing person?"

He hoped the question didn't make him sound guilty.

"Oh yes, many times," she replied.

"I've always wondered, where do you start?"

"The same as with anything, we start at the beginning."

"Is it that simple?" he asked.

"It can be. First, we check where the person was last seen and establish whether anyone or anything strange happened around the time of the disappearance. We always find clues along the way which we follow. I guess that's what I mean by starting at the beginning, we have to trace things backwards."

"I see," replied Edward, the cogs in his brain already turning. "Well, thank you. I guess it's time I went back to bed."

He turned to Claudette. "I'll check on Nicky."

"Thank you, Edward," she replied. "I'll make PC O'Brien a cup of tea before she leaves. Sleep well."

"And you Claudette. Goodnight PC O'Brien, sorry to have caused so much bother."

"No trouble Edward, take care."

Once in the safety of his bedroom, Edward took out the clues and laid them on his bed. The two sweet wrappers (the lettering on both unclear), the postcard, the newspaper article and the tiny piece of paper left by the old lady.

He read the newspaper article again and a wave of panic washed over him as he came to the final sentence.

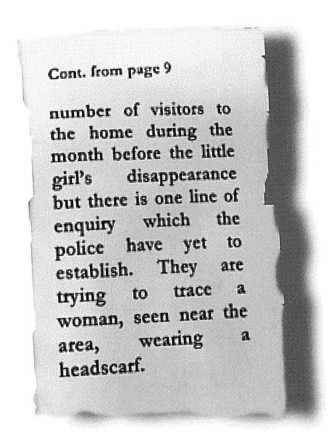

Cont. from page 9

number of visitors to the home during the month before the little girl's disappearance but there is one line of enquiry which the police have yet to establish. They are trying to trace a woman, seen near the area, wearing a headscarf.

A picture of the old lady in the garden began to form, she'd been wearing a kind of headscarf. He thought about what the police officer had said about strange people or events happening around the time of someone's disappearance. Mrs Cabbage was definitely strange.

He picked up the tiny piece of paper she'd left and studied it carefully. He didn't understand, but it had to be a clue and needed following. The police officer was right, he'd have to start at the beginning.

Chapter Eleven
Bedtime

Aunty H took Nicky by the hand and led him towards the main building. As they walked, he snuggled in. She smelt lovely, a mixture of washing powder, oranges and sweet peas.

The conversation with Cucumber had been disturbing and he wanted to ask Aunty H about it, even though the little girl had warned him not to. There was something comforting about Aunty H, as though he'd always known her. An image of his mother flashed across his mind as she smiled down at him.

"Does everyone live in here, Aunty H?"

"We do," she smiled. "All of us except Mrs M, she lives in the caravan because she snores, very loudly. This way we all get a good night's sleep!" Aunty H chuckled.

Nicky examined the dilapidated building.

"What a mess!" He glanced up at her, hoping he hadn't sounded too rude. "I'm sorry. I just mean I'm not sure I'd want to live here."

"It's a lovely home Nicky, you wait and see, I think you'll be happy with your accommodation," and with that, she opened the door and they stepped inside.

Nicky's mouth gaped.

The enormous entrance hall was the most comfortable living room he'd ever seen, and it took a few moments to take it all in. They'd stuffed sagging sofas full of cushions, creating a riot of colour against the dull and faded fabric of the furniture. Pot plants stood majestically all over the room, exotic, grand and splendid, some almost reaching to the ceiling. A multitude of rugs, collected from all over the world, covered the floor and every bookcase was jam-packed. It looked as though every book would tumble if even one was moved and Nicky wondered whether anyone dared to read to them.

Newspapers and travel magazines were stacked high on

tables dotted around the room, some of which had been attacked with a pair of scissors, pictures roughly snipped from their pages. On the floor, a large pot of glue and a brush lay near a pile of comics that had met the same fate.

Under the front window, toys spilling from inside, stood an enormous cupboard circled by a rainbow of bean bags.

"I see what you mean, it's a wonderful mess!" Nicky grinned.

"It is," Aunty H agreed. "Us oldies love the papers, especially the crosswords, and we keep them until they're completed. The children have done a good job tidying their toys away but there's no point making too much effort, they'll only get them out again tomorrow!" Aunty H squeezed his hand. "Despite the untidiness, you won't find a speck of dust, we keep it spotlessly clean."

"It's brilliant," he said. "At my house, we have to tidy our toys away as soon as we've finished playing with them. They have to be in alphabetical order too, its educational Mummy says. Edward's always having to help me with that bit." Nicky paused. "I hope he's okay, my brother I mean. I thought I'd only be away for a few hours."

"But you left him a note, didn't you?"

Briefly, a shadow passed across Aunty H's face.

"Yes, but what if he hasn't found it, what if he's already

called the police?"

Aunty H turned towards him.

"Whatever do you mean?" she sounded alarmed. "Why would he call the police?"

"No reason," he replied hastily. "I guess I'm just tired. I don't know what I'm talking about."

Aunty H's expression changed, and she laughed.

"There's nothing to worry about," she said, crossing the room to a door in the far corner. "Come and have a look in here."

The door led to a patchwork dormitory. Eleven neatly made beds stood in two rows each covered with a different coloured patchwork duvet. They'd hung patchwork curtains at the huge windows and dotted patchwork rugs on the floor. Aunty H pointed to the nearest patchwork bed.

"That's yours," she said.

It was beautiful, a bright blue patchwork duvet with gold stars covered it and folded at the bottom lay a multi-coloured knitted blanket. Nicky was pleased to see Harriet curled on top, gently snoring.

"Please can she sleep with me tonight, Aunty H?" he asked, expecting her to say no. Mummy would never allow a dog on a bed.

"If you'd like her to Nicky, that would be fine," Aunty

H replied.

He wondered if Harriet was a good guard dog as his thoughts strayed back to Mrs M, a thought which made him shiver.

Aunty H noticed.

"Are you cold Nicky?"

"No," he replied. "Where is Mrs M?"

"Oh, she'll be in her caravan. You won't see her until tomorrow. I expect she'll want to speak to you but there's nothing to worry about."

His tummy knotted. He didn't want to spend any terrifying time with her and hoped Aunty H would stay with him.

"Aunty H-"

"No more questions, Nicky, it's late and the other children will be here soon. You'll find the bathroom through there," she pointed at a patchwork door. "Your pyjamas, toothbrush and flannel are waiting for you."

Nicky obediently headed to the bathroom, brushed his teeth, and snuggled into his pyjamas. When he returned, Aunty H was waiting for him.

"You look great Nicky, come on, in you get," she patted the sheet.

As Nicky climbed in, Aunty H pulled the covers up and

was tucking him in when they heard a commotion outside.

"Get ready! The Flaming Cycles are about to enter the building," she grinned.

They arrived still in their boiler suits, chatting and laughing as they changed. Aunty H followed them around picking up items of discarded clothing and then, one by one, they clambered into bed. Aunty H tucked each one in, whispering gently as she stroked their hair and kissed them on the forehead.

Finally, she came to Nicky.

"Sleep well, sweetie, you've got an exciting day tomorrow."

"Yes." he replied nervously, and before he could stop himself asked, "When am I going home?"

"Don't worry about that, Nicky. Everything will become clear in the morning."

Leaning over, she kissed him on the forehead. "Sleep well, little man."

She turned and walked towards the bedroom door and, switching off the light, whispered in the darkness.

"Goodnight my precious lambs, now remember you promised me there'd be no talking tonight, it's lights out and you need to have a good sleep for tomorrow."

Nicky stared at the ceiling, waiting for his eyes to adjust

to the dark. He wanted to ask more questions but there was no sound and he couldn't bring himself to break the silence. Turning onto his side, he pulled the covers over his head and then dug a little hole so he could peek out.

In the far corner, he noticed a light coming from the bed with the yellow patchwork cover. Cucumber had a large pot of glue and a brush and appeared to be sticking cuttings into a tatty book. Nicky spied on her while picking his nose until she spotted him. She flashed him with an angry scowl and stuck her tongue out before turning away.

Minutes later, some of the children began gently snoring. He couldn't help but think about his brother, wondering when he'd see him again. Harriet stretched and wandered up the bed, tucking her warm body next to his. It made him feel better with the puppy by his side and, putting his arm around her, waited for sleep to come.

Eventually, it did.

Chapter Twelve
Plans

The next morning Mrs M sat at the small, rectangular dining table in her caravan. It was strewn with fabric, sequins, and in the middle, a large sewing machine. Bernard was perched opposite making adjustments to a bright blue boiler suit. He'd made many over the years but was struggling with this one, time was short and there were still sequins to add.

"This is such a lot of trouble to go to for just one show," moaned Mrs M as she tucked into an enormous box of

Turkish Delight.

Bernard smiled to himself.

"Yes, such a lot of trouble M, you look rushed off your feet!"

Holding up the top part of the costume, he checked to see if the sleeves were even.

"I am busy," she snapped defensively, "it's all on my shoulders. I am in charge!"

"Yes dear, but you're not the only one who's got a lot on their mind," he replied gently.

"It's got to be a sell-out," she said, staring at the box of Turkish Delight, deep in her own thoughts. "But at least once it's over, all we need to do is get out of here as quickly as possible."

"Faster than lightning," mumbled Bernard in agreement, pins poking from his mouth where he held them.

"It requires organisation, especially in dealing with the boy, but I'm good at that."

Her eyes narrowed, making her look like a cat about to pounce on some poor unsuspecting rat. Then, quick as a flash, her expression changed, and she smiled.

"I'm excited about our holiday. I hear Southend is marvellous. We could all do with a break and you, Bernard, need it more than any of us!" She turned her gaze on him. "I caught you napping yesterday afternoon, quite out of character. Are you okay?"

"Yes, yes I am," he replied. "I haven't been sleeping well but once it's all over, I can relax."

"You can," she agreed, taking another Turkish Delight from the box.

"As long as no one comes looking for the little lad before we've gone," he sounded nervous.

"They won't, his mother's away and that au pair, Claudette, is so busy dreaming about being one of those celebrity things it'll take years for her to notice. Cassie did a good job. Edward will have found the postcard and stuck his head back into a book. He'll be enjoying the peace and quiet without that little scrap getting in his way."

"I hope you're right. Did you read about the girl in the newspaper? Georgia May George? The people caring for her didn't notice she'd gone for a month!"

Mrs M chuckled again.

"There you go, by the time they've worked it out we'll be long gone, we've got nothing to worry about," she said, a satisfied smile on her face.

"Are you sure?" Bernard glanced at her again.

"I know what you're talking about," she snapped.

"You're talking about the newspaper, about the woman wearing a headscarf."

"Exactly!" he replied.

"Lots of people wear headscarves," she said firmly.

"Not old lady cleaning ones, not these days. It's kind of gone out of fashion."

"Stop worrying," she snapped, putting an end to the conversation. "We're going anyway, we've got no other choice and with all this nonsense in the newspaper, it couldn't come at a better time."

"Okay, okay," he said, knowing not to push the conversation further.

Mrs M continued. "The hospital is crumbling and we can't afford the repairs, everything's in place. We just need to get through today."

"And then we'll be off on another adventure!"

"Exactly, Bernard, it'll be like the good old days. I can't wait to blow the cobwebs away. We've been mouldering here too long."

She selected another Turkish Delight.

For a while, the sound of Mrs M chomping filled the caravan. Despite the mountain she'd consumed, she was still hungry. Nicky was due for his breakfast and she was looking forward to it. She giggled to herself.

Bernard studied her, puzzled by the sound but decided it was best not to ask. Reaching inside his waistcoat for his pocket watch he pulled out a dove.

"I wondered where I'd put that," he said, kissing the top of its head.

Mrs M eyeballed him and then marched to the door.

"Bernard, please have a rest. We can't have you falling asleep in the middle of the finale. I'll finish the costume."

"Thank you. I think I will put my feet up."

Bernard stood and popped the dove back in his pocket.

"And Bernard," she glowered.

"Yes, dear," he turned at the door.

"Never bring another flea-bitten, scruffy, piece of vermin into my caravan or it'll go in a pie!"

"No dear, I mean yes dear!" he said to the door which had been slammed in his face. "Sorry."

Underneath the caravan, Cucumber had heard the conversation and was once more scribbling in her picture diary. To begin with, she was excited when they'd mentioned going to the seaside, but her excitement had faded when they'd talked about the postcard. She knew Edward hadn't found it, that he probably hadn't stuck his head in a book and, at that very minute, was probably calling the police.

Cucumber groaned, if only she hadn't gone to Apple Blossom Crescent and if only Harriet hadn't licked the postcard. Well, she thought, she'd have to do something about it, she'd have to stop Edward from picking up the telephone.

It was time for Mrs Cabbage to put in another appearance!

Chapter Thirteen
The Sign

Waking early, Edward dressed in the fancy-dress costume he'd borrowed from his mother and saluted his reflection. He hoped he'd blend into his surroundings wearing army camouflage; either that or he'd stand out like a sore thumb. He remembered his mother wearing it to a party; it had been tight on her which meant he'd only had to roll the arms and legs up to make it fit.

Pulling the rucksack onto his shoulders, he crept through the house and popped a note in front of the television set. No doubt it would be the first thing Claudette saw when she finally woke.

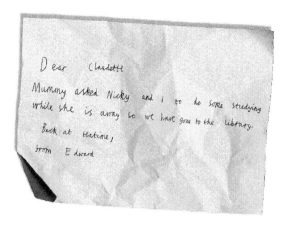

Dear Claudette

Mummy asked Nicky and I to do some studying while she is away so we have gone to the library.

Back at teatime,

from Edward

When he'd thought of it, in the middle of the night, he'd been very pleased with himself. The boys often visited after school so it wasn't too out of character and hopefully wouldn't raise any suspicion, at least he hoped it wouldn't. Either way, there was no turning back and, as he strolled down Apple Blossom Crescent towards the bus stop, he couldn't help but feel excited about the adventure ahead.

Hopping onto the bus, he could tell he'd impressed the driver.

"Nice outfit," he said. "Are you on a secret mission?"

"Sort of," replied Edward blushing.

The bus journey was far too quick and in no time at all Edward was standing in front of the library. Hovering at the entrance, he was just wondering what to do, when a familiar voice called his name. He tried to ignore it but it called again.

"Hey, Ed!"

Pulling the cap from his head, Edward turned and grinned at his best friend.

"Hey, Gary," he replied, "are you doing the science project?"

"Nah, not yet, got a few weeks still."

Gary stood next to Edward, appearing not to notice his friend's peculiar outfit.

"You going tonight?" Gary asked, pointing at the enormous poster plastered on a wall on the opposite side of the street.

"It'll be amazing, my Mum's taking me and Barry."

Gary looked at his friend while Edward stared at the poster. He'd seen it before, but where?

"Maybe…"

Gary prattled on as Edward tried to think.

"It'd be great for you to see that magician, Mum says he's brilliant, remembers him from when she was young. She said he must be ancient by now. Might be your last chance to see him, Ed. My Mum says…"

Edward stopped listening. He'd remembered where he'd seen the poster. It was the same image as the one on the front of the booklet that had fallen out of Mrs M's shopping trolley. When he'd handed it back to her, he'd caught a brief glimpse but at the time thought nothing of it.

"My Mum says it's nice that the old building is being used again. She remembers when it was a hospital. She thinks it's a shame it's being sold. She thinks they'll turn it into flats or offices or something even more boring, if that's possible. My Dad says-"

"What did you say?" Edward turned to face his friend, something in Gary's non-stop chatter rang a loud, clanging bell.

"About what?" Gary asked, sounding confused.

"About it being a hospital and about it being sold," replied Edward. "Do you know what it was called?"

"I think my Mum said it was Railway Community Hospital, you know, 'cos it's on Station Road."

Gary noticed the odd look on his friend's face. "You okay Ed?"

"Brilliant thanks, I had a sweet the other day and you've just reminded me of something. Anyway, what about the sold bit?"

"I think even you can work that out, dummy!"

Edward gazed across the street, he hadn't noticed before but there was a 'For Sale' sign nailed to the front gate, the same gate Mrs Cabbage was stumbling from.

"Oh! My! Days!" Edward cried and then, remembering his friend was standing next to him added. "Is that the time? I'd better get going Gary, but I'll definitely speak to my Mum."

"Talking of Mums," Gary said. "I'd better be off. I said I'd met mine at the car park ten minutes ago. Maybe see you later?"

Edward didn't say goodbye. He was too busy watching Mrs Cabbage as she sprinted across the road and boarded the waiting bus.

"Yeah, maybe," he replied distractedly.

The police officer had been right. By starting at the beginning, he'd been able to trace the clues to one location and one person.

But now what?

He couldn't go bowling into the old hospital and accuse Mrs Cabbage of being involved in his brother's disappearance. He didn't know who or what was inside and it might be dangerous. There was also the possibility that she was innocent. A few small clues didn't exactly amount to proof of her being a criminal mastermind.

No, he needed more evidence; he needed to find a way

to sneak into the old hospital. If his brother was inside, he could either rescue him or, if things got sticky, call the police.

He studied the poster again, and a plan began to form.

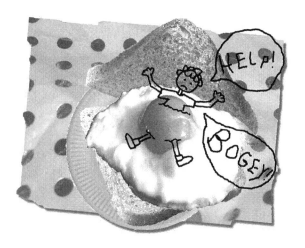

Chapter Fourteen
Breakfast with The Boss

As soon as she heard the reluctant TAP TAP, Mrs M dramatically swung the door of the caravan open and greeted Nicky with a smile, the first she'd ever given him.

"Nicky, I'm so glad you're here, please come in."

Her eyes narrowed like a wily fox about to pounce on a plump chicken.

Aunty H stood behind Mrs M's prey and gently pushed his reluctant body into the caravan.

"Enjoy your breakfast my lovely, make sure you fill yourself up," she said.

The caravan was the same as the old hospital building, grubby and unloved from the outside but inside, spotlessly clean and homely.

Nicky could see the table was set for his breakfast, one knife, one fork, and one napkin and, while hovering at the mouth of Mrs M's lair, he wondered what to do. Since waking he'd been frantically coming up with excuses, 'Sorry Mrs M I've got a tummy ache,' or, 'Sorry Mrs M I'm allergic to food,' but now he was standing in front of her, all escape plans escaped him.

"I was thinking you could have a fried egg sandwich for breakfast, but you might want something else?"

"Thank you, Mrs M," his voice was small and unsure. "That would be lovely."

"Are you thirsty? I've got lots of lovely things, lemon lump, strawberry slime, or maybe you'd like some grapefruit goo?"

Nicky didn't like the sound of any of them.

"Could I have some lemon lump please?" he said, hoping it didn't taste as gross as it sounded.

Mrs M took a large jug from the fridge and placed a glass on the kitchen counter. As she lifted the jug, Nicky saw her move a finger to her nose and poke about in her nostril. Then, using the same hand, she held the glass, steadying it as she poured.

Nicky took the glass and examined the thick yellow sludge. Thin green strands of fibre were suspended in the gloop and round the rim, hideous greasy smears of congealed snot. There was no way he'd be able to take a sip without gagging.

"Thank you," he said weakly.

"I'm sorry Nicky, please excuse my manners, make yourself comfortable." Mrs M gestured towards the table.

Clambering onto the bench, he shuffled into position, sitting as straight as he could, eager to make a good impression.

"I'm so delighted to have you here. I rarely have guests," she said, flipping the egg over in the frying pan.

Nicky watched out of the corner of his eye. Her voice was confusingly friendly, but there was something about her manner that conveyed a different story.

"Thank you," he replied, not sure what else to say.

With her back to him, he couldn't be sure but it looked suspiciously like she was picking her nose again. The same hand then held the bread as she buttered it. Nicky dreaded the green slime that, no doubt, had attached itself to his breakfast.

"Would you like some sauce?" she asked.

Yes, he thought, he hated fried egg sandwiches without tomato ketchup.

"No, thank you," he replied, hoping to avoid further bogey contamination.

With a knife in one hand, she used the other for more nasal investigation before cutting the sandwich in half. He couldn't believe his mother had chosen such a revolting cleaning lady!

"Do you know why you're here, Nicky?" she asked.

"Yes…no…I mean I don't know, not really, to begin with, I thought you were gymnasts…"

"That's sort of true, a lot of us have trained to a high level in gymnastics," she explained.

"Sounds very…interesting."

"I would prefer the word entertaining rather than interesting," her eyes glittered wickedly. "Interesting is not a very interesting word, is it?" she said spikily.

Nicky blushed and stared at the table. He hoped he hadn't upset her.

After a few seconds of silence, Nicky glanced up as she picked her nose for the fourth time. A long stringy bogey pinged out onto her finger, making his stomach churn.

"We have the most amazing show Nicky, a most spectacular show, something that will make people's eyes pop out of their heads." She turned to face him, fixing him with a piercing stare. "But we need your help."

"My help?" he repeated. "I can't help! I can't even ride a motorbike!"

"But you can Nicky, I've seen you practising. You have the skills and we'll show you how to use them. Nicky, haven't you always wanted to be a star?"

For a moment, Nicky no longer feared her. As her eyes bore into his, he believed she could see inside his brain, as though she knew everything he'd ever wanted.

"Oh yes," he sighed. "It's all I've ever dreamt of."

"Well, with a lot of hard work, dedication and concentration, not to mention luck, we'll have you ready by tonight."

"Tonight?" he whispered.

"Yes, tonight," she confirmed.

The spell was broken as fear, shock, excitement, wonder and amazement fireworked through his body.

Mrs M placed his sandwich in front of him where a bogey from her finger had attached itself to the edge of the plate. Nicky spotted it straight away and his tummy flew up and over. He wasn't sure whether he felt ill because of the sandwich or the performance.

Mrs M settled opposite.

"Now eat up, Nicky. Remember what Aunty H said. We need you to be nice and strong. You've got a lot of work to do to be ready in time."

Nicky looked down at the slimy sandwich, its edges glistening with strings of snot.

"Come on, Nicky!" she barked, making him jump.

Slowly he lifted the sandwich to his mouth and, closing his eyes, took a big bite. Best behaviour, he thought, as he held the food in his mouth, too afraid to chew.

"Good boy."

He detected a slight giggle in her voice.

"Now get that down you and I'll fetch Bernard and Cassie. They'll show you what to do."

"Mrs M," he said, trying to talk politely with a mouth full of bogey sandwich.

"Yes, Nicky, do you have a question?" she asked, rising from the table.

"What do you do?"

"Me?" she said. "Isn't it obvious? I'm in charge. I'm the ringleader!"

Again, the glittering sparkle in her eyes and the haughty expression. She was so close he could see right up her nose, not a clump or string of bogey remained.

"Ringleader?" Nicky gulped.

Mrs M laughed. "Isn't it obvious? That's why they call me The Boss!"

"Oh yes," he replied, trying to hide the thoughts now flooding into his brain.

"Anyway, we haven't got time to sit and chit chat all day. I'll find them and then you can get on with the training."

After she'd gone, Nicky stared at the egg sandwich and his full glass, trying to digest what she'd told him. As soon as she'd said she was the ringleader he'd pictured the ones in the stories his brother read him. Masterminds of evil gangs who slunk around committing crimes and being bad eggs.

Cassie and Cucumber had been clear in telling him they were secret and both seemed fearful of the police. He thought back to what Cucumber had said about him living at the old hospital, about it being his home and began to worry. He wanted to go back to Apple Blossom Crescent, to Edward, his Mummy, and even to Claudette. He didn't want to be part of their gang and didn't want to live a life of crime. The other thing he didn't want to do was eat a sandwich full of bogey.

Nicky jumped up and tipped the contents of his glass

into the nearest pot plant. Then he began searching the caravan. Minutes ticked by and he still hadn't found anywhere to hide the sandwich so, in the end, he was forced to take drastic action. When Mrs M, Bernard and Cassie appeared seconds later, he hoped he didn't look too guilty.

"Well done Nicky, good eating." Mrs M nodded with approval at his empty plate.

"Thank you, Mrs M. It was delicious," he lied.

"Are you ready, young man?" Bernard grinned broadly. "I hear Mrs M has explained everything?"

Nicky returned his smile while the sandwich which he'd stuffed down the back of his pants gently warmed his bottom.

"She has, I'm beginning to get the idea," he replied, hoping they couldn't hear the terror in his voice.

Chapter Fifteen
The Grouchers

Ding dong!

Claudette groaned.

"Who's that!?" she asked the empty room as she paused the television, popped another chocolate in her mouth and impatiently thumped down the stairs to the front door.

At the bottom, a piece of paper lay on the doormat, her name scrawled across it.

As she read, her heart began to flutter and her cheeks

flushed a deep shade of pink.

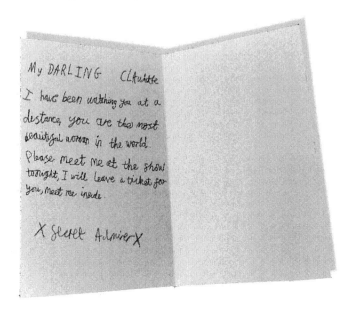

It had turned Edward's tummy when he'd added the kisses but was sure Claudette would fall for it, hook, line and sinker.

After ringing the doorbell at Number 8, he'd hidden behind a fir tree at Number 13 for a few minutes and then darted down the street to the phone box.

Back at Number 8, Claudette had settled back on the sofa when…

Beep!Twing! Beep!Twing!

She thought of the note, maybe her secret admirer was calling?

"Hello?" she said into the phone.

"Hello!" replied the high, squeaky, breathless voice on the other end of the line.

"Can I help you?" Claudette asked.

"I hope so," wheezed the voice. "This is Mrs Tuttle, Gary and Barry's mother. I was wondering if the boys would like to have a sleepover at our house tonight?" Edward asked.

"Oh, um, I…who are Gary and Barry?" how funny she thought, children with rhyming names!

"They're at school together, they're best friends, Gary is the short one, always looks a complete mess and Barry is the one with the terrible squint." Edward tried not to laugh as he imitated Mrs Tuttle.

Claudette vaguely remembered them, noisy little boys she thought to herself.

"Oh, yes, they talk a lot," and then remembering she was speaking to their mother added, "I mean talk a lot in a good way."

"Yes, they do," Edward agreed as a giggle tickled the back of his throat. "So, I'll collect them from the library and drop them home in the morning. Don't worry, it won't be too early, I'm sure you'd appreciate a lie-in. Your job sounds very demanding."

"Yes, it is Mrs Tuttle, how kind of you," Claudette agreed.

"With the boys out for the evening, you should make the most of it. Maybe you could go out tonight?" Edward couldn't resist checking if his plan was working. "I expect a lovely girl like you has thousands of admirers?"

He placed his hand over the receiver so she didn't hear the splutter as the giggle forced itself up his neck into his mouth.

"Actually, Mrs Tuttle I do have a date tonight." Claudette's cheeks redden.

"Smashing! Goodbye then," replied Edward, slamming the receiver down and crumpling into fits of laughter.

"Goodbye," Claudette said to the empty phone line.

Earlier in the day, staring at the poster at the bottom of Station Road, Edward had come up with a simple plan. He was going to the show! With everyone distracted by the performance, he'd have the perfect opportunity to sneak into the old hospital, find Nicky, and get back in time to see Bernardo The Brillianto!

However, on the bus journey home, he remembered his mother was due back that evening and would want to know where he and his brother were. A flash of inspiration and he'd come up with the fake invitation from Mrs Tuttle to the sleepover, problem one solved!

The second problem was the lack of a back-up plan. If things went horribly wrong, what would he do? Thankfully, it didn't take long to work that out too. He would lure both his mother and Claudette to the show.

The secret admirer had been an obvious choice for Claudette but his mother would be more difficult. Eventually, he decided he'd have to deal with that issue later.

In the meantime, he needed to buy three tickets, one for him, one for Claudette and one for his mother. That was the third problem, he needed to get to his money box in his bedroom without Claudette seeing.

As the bus pulled up to Apple Blossom Crescent Edward had another flash of inspiration!

The driveway of Number 16 was empty so, checking left and right, Edward leant against the garage door of the Groucher's house.

CLUNK! *GRIND!*

The door lifted and Edward grimaced. It was too noisy, and he worried if he tried again, one of the neighbours would come dashing out to investigate or, worse still, call the police.

Edward lay flat on the driveway and peered into the blackness of the garage. The gap between the ground and the door looked just about big enough to squeeze through, but halfway under, there was an almighty

SCREECH!

Frantically he clawed at the concrete while shoving his body through to the other side.

BANG!

That was close thought Edward, facing the huge metal door that had nearly slammed him in half. He waited while his heart rate returned to a steady beat and then started searching.

Shelves stuffed with bottles and jars of nuts, bolts and screws lined the walls and in the far corner, propped against the wall, was a ladder. Edward took it down and was wondering how to escape when the sound of a car pulled onto the driveway. A minute later and he could hear the familiar din of the Groucher's arguing as they entered the house.

With no way back through the garage door and the Groucher's inside, he knew there wasn't a hope of escaping carrying a ladder. Reluctantly, he put it back where he'd first found it and snuck over to the internal door. Gingerly, he opened it, one millimetre at a time.

AAAGGHHH! Mr Groucher was standing in front of him.

"What would you like in your sandwich, Margery?" Mr Groucher shouted to Mrs Groucher.

"Shrimp paste!" came the yelled reply.

Edward peered through the tiny crack in the door.

Ring! Ring!   Ring! Ring!

"Geoffrey, it's the telephone," screeched Mrs Groucher. "I can't hear my animal programme."

Mr Groucher rushed off towards the living room.

"Yes Mother, it was lovely to see you too."

Edward could hear Mr Groucher as he tried to compete with the blaring television.

"Yes, I'll see you next week as usual," he yelled.

With both Grouchers occupied, Edward took a risk and crept into the kitchen. The hideous aroma of shrimp paste filled his nostrils with its foul stench making him gag.

In the living room, he could see Mrs Groucher, feet up, watching telly and Mr Groucher, talking on the telephone with his back to the door.

"Yes, Mother I will make sure I see the doctor. I agree it is a very unsightly rash," he bawled.

"Oh, do we have to go through that again!" yelled Mrs Groucher.

"Yes, well, I can't quite reach it so I've tried some ointment and a shoehorn."

He ignored his wife and continued talking to his mother.

Edward began to giggle, quickly clamping his hand over his mouth.

"Geoffrey, where's that sandwich?" Mrs Groucher snapped. "And don't talk about your bottom before lunch!"

Edward screwed up his face. The thought of Mr Groucher's behind was rather a repulsive one.

"Sorry mother, can you wait a moment?"

Placing his hand over the mouthpiece he hissed at his

wife.

"My mother is concerned about my medical condition, Margery. Please be quiet."

Mrs Groucher rose from her chair.

"I'm going to the toilet. I'd like my sandwich when I get back."

"Yes, Mother." continued Mr Groucher. "I'm so excited about the show tonight. I remember when you took me. I'll call tomorrow and tell you all about it but I must go, Margery is a little irritable. I expect she's hungry. Goodbye."

Edward was trapped!

With Mr Groucher on his way back to the kitchen, he cast an eye about, desperate to find somewhere to hide.

"Geoffrey, there's no toilet paper!" screamed Mrs Groucher from the bathroom.

Mr Groucher changed direction and stormed down the hallway.

"Really Margery, it's on the shelf, didn't you notice when you came in?"

While Mr Groucher was helping his wife, Edward made a run for it, diving into the coats at the bottom by the front door.

BUZZ! BUZZ! BUZZ!

Cripes, thought Edward holding his breath and hoping Mr Groucher didn't spot his feet poking out of the coats.

"Yes?" Mr Groucher enquired of the person standing outside.

A strident, high-pitched voice rang out.

"I am the Dealer's cleaner. I understand you have a ladder. I'd like to borrow it, please."

From the bathroom, Mrs Groucher began complaining again.

"Geoffrey, who is it? I need to wipe my bottom!"

Mr Groucher reddened.

"Please excuse my wife." Mr Groucher's reply sounded flustered.

"If you can carry it over to Number 8, that would be helpful," replied the visitor, "and it might give your wife time to finish what she's doing."

Embarrassed, Mr Groucher was pleased to have an excuse to leave the house.

"I'll get it straight away," he confirmed.

As soon as he'd gone Edward flung himself out of the front door and raced towards the fir trees at Number 13. Mrs Cabbage and Mr Groucher emerged from the garage; the ladder slung over his shoulder.

"Just pop it at the front please," she instructed as Mr

Groucher trotted behind her.

From inside Number 16, Mrs Groucher was trying to get her husband's attention.

"Geoffrey! Geoffrey! I can't sit here all day!"

As Mr Groucher walked past the fir tree, Edward heard him muttering.

"Well, get your own toilet paper then, you lazy lump."

"Pardon?" shouted Mrs Groucher from inside the house.

"Nothing dear, I'm on my way," he called back, slamming the door behind him.

Phew, that was close, thought Edward, but he wasn't out of danger. A chill ran through him as he remembered the caller. What on earth was Mrs Cabbage up to?

Chapter Sixteen
The Costume

Following the hideous breakfast with Mrs M, Bernard and Cassie had collected Nicky, and the three of them were now standing in front of an enormous trampoline. It was bigger than the biggest trampoline Nicky had ever seen and he guessed it had enough bounce to send him rocketing into space.

"Are you ready, little fellow?" Bernard smiled and his eyes twinkled.

"I promise you'll love it," Cassie said.

Despite his concerns, Nicky couldn't help but feel

excited. At home, he'd spent hours tumbling and flipping, bouncing and somersaulting in front of an imaginary audience and now he was only hours away from performing in front of a real one. Part of him couldn't wait and the other part was petrified.

"Wow!" he said. "That's incredible!"

"If you think that's good, have a look over there." Cassie pointed towards the gap in the hedge.

In the field where he'd first seen the Flaming Cycles perform, an enormous tent was being constructed. Mrs S, Mr G and Mr W were lugging large sheets of metal across the site while The Flaming Cycles stood on each other's shoulders, attaching tarpaulin to the frame. Colin saw him and waved.

"Don't get distracted," said Bernard.

"What?" asked Nicky.

"I just mean, if you think about the tent too much, it might make you nervous," he laughed.

It was too late, it already had.

Cassie leapt onto the trampoline and started bouncing. As she flew up and over, Nicky noticed bandages on her arm and leg.

"What happened to Cassie?" he asked.

"There was a slight accident, Nicky, that's why we need

your help."

"Because of an accident?" Nicky sounded horrified. "But what if the same thing happens to me?"

"It won't," Bernard replied, trying to sound reassuring.

"And it wasn't so bad that Cassie can't perform, it's just that she must stay on her bike rather than help me. That's what I need you to do, Nicky. Do you think you can help me?"

Nicky's brow furrowed.

"Help you?"

By now Cassie had flipped off the trampoline and joined them.

"It's the end bit, our little secret," she said, winking at Bernard. "I don't have the strength, and if I were to miss it, the act wouldn't work."

Bernard cut in. "But you needn't worry, Nicky. You won't miss it; I'll be there to catch you."

"Do you promise?" Nicky asked doubtfully.

"I do Nicky, but you need confidence, confidence in me, but also in yourself."

Nicky smiled weakly.

"I know!" said Bernard suddenly remembering, "I'd completely forgotten until now!"

Nicky hoped whatever it was would remove all doubt

from his mind.

"Your costume!"

"My costume?"

"Yes," Bernard replied. "I'm not ready until I'm wearing mine. I promise you'll feel invincible. I made it myself. I've put magic in it, you'll see when you put it on!"

Nicky looked doubtfully at him again.

"I guess."

"Aunty H has it, pop inside and when you get back Cassie and I can explain everything, even the secret bit."

It was Bernard's turn to wink at Cassie.

As he walked towards the main building, Nicky thought about the egg sandwich he'd hidden in the back of his pants. It was making his bottom very soggy and he couldn't wait to get rid of it. He went straight to the dormitory and was about to enter when he heard voices.

"But are you sure we'll get away with it?" asked Aunty H.

"We have to." Mrs M's reply sounded agitated. "I know what I'm doing, and so does Bernard. Nicky will disappear and then, once the tents are down, so will we."

Harriet padded over to where he was crouching behind the sofa. She could smell the fried egg sandwich and began pawing at him.

"Yes, Harriet," Nicky whispered. "Give me a minute."

Harriet didn't understand and started whining just as the door of the dormitory creaked open. Nicky raced back towards the front door where he began stroking her, pretending he'd just walked in.

Aunty H was the first to appear.

"Hello Nicky, what are you doing here?"

"Bernard said I should come and ask you for the costume. He said it would give me confidence. He said there's magic in it."

"Oh, there is Nicky, lots of it," replied Aunty H. "Come with me, I'll show you."

Mrs M appeared from the dormitory and made a bee-line for him.

"Remember Nicky, you've got to get this right. You mustn't let me down!"

"I won't, Mrs M," he replied nervously as she swept out of the room.

Aunty H held out her hand, and he raced towards her, holding it tightly as they escaped to the safety of the dormitory.

"Ignore her," Aunty H said. "She's always like it before a show; it's the theatrics coming out."

Nicky didn't know what the theatrics were but didn't

like the sound of them.

"Can I put the costume on now please, Aunty H?" he asked, while Harriet sat at his feet wagging her tail, desperate for whatever treat he had for her.

"Yes, it's through there," she said, pointing towards the bathroom.

Harriet bounded after him and greedily ate the scraps of egg sandwich he fed her. Then, once he'd washed his bottom, he dressed in the bright blue boiler suit that Bernard had made and picked up the glittering helmet.

For the first time, he noticed the name written on the back in gold sequins; it said 'Clive'. Nicky smiled, it was a manly name and as he stepped back to admire his reflection in the bathroom mirror, he puffed his chest out and a wave of pride washed over him. He looked different, more grown-up than in real life. Bernard had been right, he felt fantastic and possibly even a little invincible, there really was magic in the costume.

"Does it fit okay? We need to get you back to Bernard and Cassie," Aunty H called through the door.

"I'm on my way," he called back.

As he stepped from the bathroom, Aunty H beamed at him, clasping her hands to her chest.

"Don't you look grown-up Nicky, so handsome."

"I do feel special," he admitted shyly.

"Come on, we mustn't keep them waiting. You've got a lot to do this afternoon but once you've finished come and find me, I'll have a slice of cake waiting."

"Thank you," he replied and started making his way back to the trampoline.

As he walked, he tried to decide whether he'd prefer to join Mrs M's criminal gang and live at the old hospital or let them make him disappear. Neither were appealing and with mounting fear, he realised he'd have to find a way of escaping. If only Edward were here, he thought, he'd know what to do.

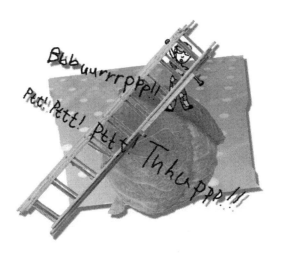

Chapter Seventeen
Operation Break-In

"Why do you need that oddball's ladder?" Mrs Cabbage snorted from underneath her shawl.

She'd been waiting with it while Edward slunk back across Apple Blossom Crescent.

"Do you mean Mr Groucher? He's not an oddball," he replied defensively.

"Isn't he?" giggled Mrs Cabbage.

Edward couldn't argue with that.

"So?" she pressed. "What are you going to do with it,

now I've got it for you?"

Edward was suspicious, why had she helped him with the ladder if she was involved in his brother's disappearance? Then he was struck by another thought, how on earth had she known he needed the ladder?

"How did you know I needed the ladder?" he asked.

"I do have eyes!" she was laughing at him. "There's a great, big gap in the garage door!"

Edward didn't like the idea of her spying on him, it made him feel very uncomfortable and he decided he needed to get rid of her.

"Sorry, I've got a lot to do and I can't stand around chatting," he said as he started wrestling with the ladder.

"Please yourself," snapped Mrs Cabbage. "I only came to check on you."

"Check on me?" Edward repeated.

"Yes, the last time we met you mentioned something about losing a brother. Extremely irresponsible in my opinion, but I thought I'd come and see if you'd found him?"

Edward was confused, he didn't have a clue what she was up to but one thing was certain, she was getting in the way of his carefully planned plan.

"Thanks, Mrs Cabbage, but everything's under control."

Edward turned, hoping to end the conversation.

"Edward!" she barked. "I only want five minutes of your time."

Edward scowled. Why wouldn't she just get the message and go away?

"Pleeeeaaasssseee," she whined, "it's important."

Edward thought for a minute. It was clear the old lady wouldn't go until he'd agreed to talk to her.

"Okay," he replied reluctantly. "But not here."

"Deal." Mrs Cabbage yelled as she dashed off around the back of Number 8.

Edward followed, lurching from side to side as he struggled through the gate with the ladder resting on his shoulder. It was a relief to put it down.

"Now where's that oddball gone?" Edward said to himself as his eyes swept the garden, trying to guess where she'd spring from this time.

He waited and watched and waited a bit more.

Then the penny dropped.

She'd tricked him, only asking about his brother to slow him down. Edward was cross with himself and needed no further proof she was in it up to her neck. How could he have fallen for it?

He checked his watch and his tummy tightened, he'd

lost valuable time and knew he had to put 'Operation Break-In' into operation immediately!

With the ladder propped against the wall of the house, he placed both hands on it and wiggled it from side to side. It crunched against the gravel, refusing to settle. Eventually, Edward decided he'd just have to go for it, regardless of how precarious the climb.

He took the first few steps up and the ladder tilted to the left while his stomach somersaulted. A wave of sickness bubbled up, and he thought his heart was thumping so loudly that it'd thump all the way out of his chest. He waited, trying to calm his nerves before placing another trembling foot on the next rung. A few more steps and he realised he'd been concentrating so hard he'd forgotten to breathe. Now he was dizzy! Gripping the ladder tightly, he gulped air in like a fish. Don't look down, don't look down, he thought over and over.

Not feeling at all brave, but aware of the minutes ticking by, he took the last few rungs to the top. By now his legs were shaking so violently that the ladder jerked beneath him. Hanging onto the edge of the second-floor balcony, he knew he'd have to move fast to stop it from crashing to the ground. So, with all his strength, he grabbed onto the railing and hauled himself over.

Landing on the paved tiles with a thud, he couldn't help but let out a tiny, "Eeekkk!"

In front of him, the french doors stood wide open and he could see the back of Claudette's head as she lounged on the sofa, watching telly and talking to herself.

"Oh, my darling," she said in a weird husky voice. "You're the most wonderful man in all the world."

As usual, she was copying the lines from a film, no doubt some boring, sloppy, kissy thing she'd seen a million times. Edward thought it sounded gross but on the bright side, it was so loud; she hadn't heard him.

The next phase of 'Operation Break-In' was tricky. The distance to the back wall where he planned to scale the Wisteria that grew up the side of the house to his third-floor bedroom window seemed far away. Was there any hope of getting past without being spotted?

Lying flat on the ground, inch by inch he started crawling across the balcony. Dressed in his army camouflage, he imagined himself on a mission, entering dangerous territory. For a while, it took his mind off the stressful situation and he almost began to enjoy himself. Then, the enemy let out an enormous belch.

Bbbuuurrrrrrppppppppp!!!!!!!!

Edward giggled before clamping his hand firmly over

his mouth. He couldn't afford to get discovered now that he'd come so far!

He waited for a few more seconds, just until he was sure the laughter had subsided and then started crawling again. But...

Ptt! Ptt! Pttt! **THHUPPP!!!**

This time the noise came from her bottom and was way funnier than the first.

Edward shoved his face into the ground, biting his lip to stop himself from laughing. His whole body shook and he could feel tears of laughter prickle his eyes but, try as he might, he couldn't stop thinking about it. To distract himself, he pictured his brother, alone and scared, and once more the reality of the situation came into sharp focus and he stopped laughing.

The last few crawls were agony as he shuffled past the open balcony door, his knees and elbows still sore from the garage door incident. Claudette was now so close he could almost smell the box of chocolates she was busily chomping through.

One final crawl and he'd safely made it to the back wall.

Above hung thick vines of Wisteria, almost branch-like. He hoped they'd be strong enough to hold him and carefully placed one foot on the thickest vine. His tummy churned once more as he prepared to climb.

Heaving himself up, he was only a few feet off the ground when he panicked. He could see over the edge of the balcony to the ground below. It was such a long way down and his arms were tiring. The vines were also becoming a problem. The higher he went, the thinner they became. But it was too late, he couldn't turn back.

Three-quarters of the way up he stopped again to catch his breath. It was a terrible mistake because once more the temptation to look down overtook him. His head swam, and he felt like he needed the toilet as shock shot through his body like a lightning bolt. In terror, he began scrabbling upwards and, although he knew he was making a lot of noise, he didn't care anymore. He just wanted to be safe, he wanted to be home.

The windowsill was close now and, with one final superhuman burst of energy, he grabbed it with one hand. Nearly there, he thought, and although he wasn't out of danger, his spirits soared.

A few more inches and his eyes were level with the window. He could see his reflection, the army cap reminding him that the most dangerous part of the mission was nearly over.

He was delighted! He'd almost done it!

But then he made another, even bigger, mistake. He took one hand from the Wisteria and saluted his reflection.

Below his feet, the vines started snapping, and he tried desperately to find something to hold onto with his free hand. But they were only the young shoots of the plant which hadn't yet attached themselves to the wall.

Desperately he tore at them, trying to save himself but it was hopeless and he knew it was only a matter of seconds before he'd plunge to the ground. His tummy flipped, and he opened his mouth wide to scream for help.

Chapter Eighteen
Unexpected Guest

Something soft brushed across Edward's face. Luckily, he'd been so scared that when he opened his mouth to scream, no sound had come out. So, with his mouth open and one hand still gripping the windowsill, he looked up and was more than a little alarmed to see Mrs Cabbage and some material hanging out of his bedroom window.

"Grab it!" she hissed.

With no time to question her, he reached up and clung onto the bedsheet, gripping it tightly as he held on for dear life.

Half pulled by Mrs Cabbage, he scrabbled up and swung through the window. He'd expected to land on the soft carpet below, but instead, something small and bony was wriggling beneath him.

"Ow!" cried Mrs Cabbage, thrashing about where she'd broken his fall.

"How did you get in here?" Edward was stunned.

"Through the back door!" she mumbled. "Now get off. I can't breathe!"

Edward tumbled off. "Didn't Claudette see you?"

"The one glued to the telly?" replied the old lady dusting herself down. "That thing wouldn't notice if a unicorn dressed as a sailor trotted past!" She laughed at her own joke.

Edward started to pace, he'd had enough, it was time for some explanations.

"I know what you're up to Mrs Cauliflower. I know you're trying to trick me."

"Cabbage!" she snapped.

"Cabbage?" he replied. "What has a cabbage got to do with it?"

"My name is Mrs Cabbage," she paused, "and as for trying to trick you, I really don't know what you're talking about. As I've already explained, I'm a busy old lady and I just want to talk to you but, before we get to that, I suggest you stop making such a dreadful noise."

She glanced towards his feet thumping backwards and forwards across the bedroom carpet. Edward looked down too. She was right; he was making a bit of a racket.

After slipping his shoes off he tucked them under his bed while wondering why he'd gone to all the trouble of borrowing the ladder and risking his life breaking in when a complete stranger had wandered past the au pair, without a second glance.

"Don't worry about all that," she sighed, as though reading his thoughts. "We need to talk about Nicky."

Edward's eyes narrowed. "How do you know my brother's name?"

An icy chill ran up and down his body.

Mrs Cabbage didn't reply.

"You know where he is, don't you?"

"No." Her voice sounded hesitant.

Edward knew she was lying.

"You'd better tell me because if you don't, I'll call the police!" Edward suddenly felt very brave.

"I can't tell you!" she was panicking. "But you've got to believe me, he's fine. More than fine, he's having the time of his life."

Inside the shawl, Cucumber grimaced, by mentioning Nicky's name she'd blown it, no longer an innocent old lady checking up on a lost boy.

"You really are a naughty old lady Mrs Cabbage, there's no way you can squirm your way out of this one. The police will be very interested when I show them the evidence I've collected."

Edward walked over to the rucksack and took out the newspaper.

"See!" he said, "I know about the little girl. I read all about it in here."

"What girl?" she sounded genuinely confused.

Edward handed her the article, but she put her hand up and pushed it away. "I'm sorry, dear. I haven't got my reading specs."

"Okay, listen to this."

As he reached the last sentence, Mrs Cabbage gasped. Until then she'd forgotten about the conversation she'd overheard between Bernard and Mrs M. At the time it hadn't seemed important, but now mention of the missing child and the lady with the headscarf terrified her.

"So," he said, laying the evidence on his bed, "I've got it all; your bus ticket, your description in the newspaper, I've even got the sweet wrappers from Railway Community Hospital. The ones you left when you took Nicky, there's no way you can deny it."

"You've got it all wrong Edward," she hissed.

"How?" Edward demanded.

"Nicky's fine, he's in the show tonight. He wants to do it and he's happy. You'll just ruin everything if you involve the police."

Edward was dumbstruck.

"He's in the show? Do you mean as a performer?"

Mrs Cabbage nodded. "Not just a performer, he's got a starring role!" Mrs Cabbage sounded oddly close to tears.

Edward didn't want to fall for another of her tricks but was starting to believe her.

"I want to see him!" he demanded.

"You can, before the performance," she hesitated again. "But one thing Edward, promise me you won't call the police."

Edward thought for a moment.

"If you don't promise I won't help you." she insisted.

Edward had no other choice, he had to agree, "Okay, but where will I find you?"

"Don't worry, I'll find you," she replied, walking towards the window. "But for goodness sakes, get a move on Edward, the ticket office opens soon!"

Then Edward watched, with some surprise, as she sprung onto the windowsill, slipped down the bedsheet, flipped over the balcony, and skidded down the ladder with amazing agility and speed. She really was very peculiar, he thought.

Grabbing his money box, he unplugged the stopper and inserted his fingers, feeling for the crisp notes before gently tweezering them through the bottom. With a wallet full of cash, he opened his laptop, created a new email address, and began typing.

To mdealer@dealer&sons

URGENT BUSINESS MEETING TONIGHT

Dear Mrs Dealer

Please excuse me but I believe you are a very brilliant business lady and I have a very interesting deal for you. Unfortunately, I will only be in the country for one evening, that is tonight.

I can't tell you about it now so please meet me at the show on Station Road at 7:00. I will leave you a ticket at the box office.

My friend says you are good at making money and are excellent at your job. I think you are the only person who is good enough for this fantastic opportunity.

I will be on my private jet this afternoon so can't reply to any questions.

Yours sincerely
Mr Importante

Edward read it back and was just about to press **SEND** when he remembered the promise he'd made his brother.

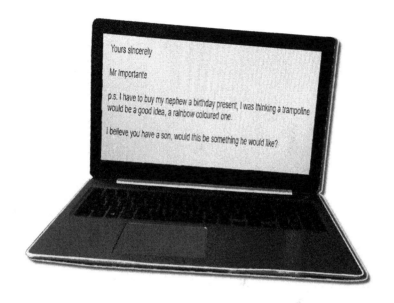

Yours sincerely

Mr Importante

p.s. I have to buy my nephew a birthday present, I was thinking a trampoline would be a good idea, a rainbow coloured one.

I believe you have a son, would this be something he would like?

He glanced towards the window but wisely decided it would be safer to leave by the stairs. When he peered into the landing, he noticed the bathroom door was closed. Claudette, no doubt, was getting ready for her date. Hooray, thought Edward, the plan was working! Sneaking out of his room he was halfway down the stairs when he remembered he'd forgotten his shoes. He turned to retrace his steps just as Claudette came bounding out of the bathroom with no clothes on!

Edward screwed his eyes up tightly while flattening himself against the carpet as he tried to erase the vision from his mind. Luckily, Claudette, distracted by her date, didn't notice a flat Edward lying on the stairs and while she was in her room, he had enough time to escape.

On the short walk to the bus stop, Edward decided not to worry about his lack of shoes. It wasn't the worst thing that had happened in the last twenty-four hours, he thought. No, that was still to come.

Chapter Nineteen
Cake

The day had flown by and it was getting late when Cassie led Nicky through the gap in the hedge. He'd worked hard but wasn't the tiniest bit tired. It was Bernard who'd struggled, taking several naps throughout the day leaving Cassie to do most of the training. The pair worked well together and, despite his mounting concern, Nicky had enjoyed every single second, so much so, he hadn't come up with an escape plan yet.

As Nicky approached the showground, he was even

more wowed by the beauty of the enormous red and gold tent. All day the others had been busy building it and now, fully constructed, it was splendid, soaring high into the sky. At the top, right in the middle, was a long streaming flag gently waving in the breeze. Nicky's heart raced and a burning sensation spread through his tummy. He inhaled deeply, trying to steady himself and for the first time saw the rest of the tiny tent village.

On the right-hand side they'd set up stalls and a ticket office, and on the left, nearest the opening in the hedge, was the performer's tent which connected to the main one. Nicky marvelled at how quickly they'd put it together.

"You okay?" asked Cassie.

"Y-y-yes, I think so," he replied in a small voice. "I hadn't expected all of this."

"I know," Cassie replied, "the first time I saw it I was absolutely astounded. The sad thing is it'll only be here for a few hours. Once the audience has gone, they'll spend all night taking it down."

"Wow!" he said. "That really is incredible, and then what?"

"We celebrate a marvellous show with some fizzy pop!"

Cassie laughed and started walking away, leaving Nicky staring at the entrance. For a minute he thought about making a dash for it, it might be his only opportunity.

"Come on, Nicky," Cassie was right behind him. "You need to keep your muscles warm or you'll get a cramp."

Reluctantly, Nicky followed her to the back of the tent.

"Cassie, can I ask you something?"

"Yeah, sure," she replied. "Fire away."

"Will I go home tonight, back to Apple Blossom Crescent?"

Cassie placed her hands on his shoulders and stared into his eyes.

"I honestly don't know Nicky, they haven't told me," she smiled warmly. "But you mustn't worry. For the next few hours, all you need to do is focus on the performance. You mustn't get distracted by anything, not the slightest, tiniest little thing. Look, there's something I should probably tell you about the accident."

Nicky looked up at her, fear in his eyes.

"It wasn't my fault, Nicky, but I wasn't concentrating. I got distracted."

Nicky saw a tear trickle down her cheek.

"And since then there hasn't been an hour I haven't thought about it. It was my dream to perform, to do what you're doing. Nicky, this will be one of the most amazing, memorable and magical nights of your life, don't let it go to waste, focus on it, nothing else."

"I know Cassie but Cucumber frightened me, she said it-"

"That's what I'm talking about Nicky, you're getting distracted by nonsense!" Cassie was serious, but she laughed, trying to cheer him up. "Cucumber's always coming up with ridiculous ideas, sneaking around and making things up. She'll get herself into a lot of trouble one of these days, really she hasn't got a clue, she's such a daydreamer."

Nicky half-smiled, still unsure.

"People are coming from all around to see us, to see you, imagine that Nicky, you mustn't let them down!"

"You're right Cassie, I promise, I won't let anyone down."

"Good," she said. "Let's do some star jumps."

As they jumped up and down, arms and legs flying in the air, Nicky gazed at the tent and gulped. He was beyond excited about the performance and there was no way he would let anyone down but he wanted to go home. He tried really hard to do what Cassie said, to concentrate, but it wouldn't work. He was sure if he had an escape plan, he'd stop worrying.

"Nicky!" a shrill voice called from behind.

Turning, he was startled to see a large mint coloured, feathered creature, walking towards him. As it got closer, the familiar face of Aunty H became clearer.

"I brought you that cake," she said.

She had large fake eyelashes, gold lipstick and sparkly gemstones around her eyes in feather shapes. Her body was squeezed into a mint green leotard with thick flesh-coloured tights covering her legs. There were mint and lemon feathers around her waist which created a skirt, and trailing down the back, longer feathers formed a tail. Her hair was set in silvery curls with enormous feathers standing proud on one side. She looked amazing.

"Wow, thank you Aunty H, I'm starving," he said, gratefully taking the enormous slice of chocolate cake covered in whipped cream and strawberries. "You look incredible!"

"Thank you, Nicky," she beamed.

"Where's mine?" whined Cassie.

"In the tent, help yourself my little darling."

Cassie ran off, keen to get a slice before the rest of the Flaming Cycles devoured it.

"How are you my little sugar lump?" Aunty H asked.

"Oh, I'm buzzing!" he replied, stuffing cake into his mouth, "but nervous too."

"You needn't be, my lovely. You just need to believe in yourself, I believe in you." She put her arm around him.

Nicky looked at her. There was definitely something about Aunty H, something that reminded him of home.

"I had a little girl you know Nicky, a daughter with curly blonde hair and a beautiful beaming smile, just like yours."

"Did you?" he replied. "Where is she?"

"She disappeared, a few years ago, and I haven't seen her since."

"Disappeared! Didn't you look for her?" Nicky was alarmed.

"Sorry Nicky, that's probably the wrong word to use. She was an adult and I couldn't stop her going. I don't think this life was for her so she went off to find a different one. I'm sorry. I didn't mean to alarm you. I only mentioned it because in some ways you remind me of her."

"Do you miss her?" he asked.

"Every day I think about her, about what she's doing and where she might be."

"I think about my Mummy."

Nicky felt tears well up, he wanted to ask her the same question he'd asked Cassie about whether he was going home.

"I'm so sorry, Nicky. I don't want to make you sad, let's

change the subject. Did you know, when I was younger, they called me 'The Canary'. I used to fly about the tent, singing and swooping; it was an amazing feeling. Unfortunately, I'm getting old and it's not as easy as it used to be. Just as well, I look more like a chicken these days!" she winked at him.

Nicky giggled, grinning at her.

"What's so funny?"

"You're the most beautiful chicken I've ever seen!"

Aunty H grinned back. "You say the nicest things Nicky, and may I say, you are the most handsome gymnast I've ever seen."

Nicky blushed. "I can't tell you how excited I am. I've always wanted to be in a show."

"Well, it won't be long now, I think it's time we got you back to Cassie."

When they found her, Cassie was tinkering with her bike, making final adjustments.

"Goodbye, Nicky." She hugged him tightly. "Break a leg!"

"Goodbye Aunty H, you too!"

He watched as she disappeared inside the tent wondering if he'd ever talk to her again. He liked her and realised he'd miss her once he'd escaped.

Chapter Twenty

Mr Importante Arrives

Edward arrived at the old hospital and headed straight for the back of the queue which already stretched halfway down Station Road. He listened to people chatting excitedly as they waited for the ticket booth to open.

"Do you remember the time they shot that giant bird from a canon and it tore through the top of the tent?" someone said.

"That must have been years ago. I'm surprised they can still do it. They must be ancient by now," someone else

151

replied.

"It wasn't a bird, was it? Thought it was a woman?" his friend asked. "But yeah, you're right, they'll be nearly past it. I bet they won't perform again."

"Unlikely, I guess that's why it'll be a sell-out, everyone's desperate to see them before they retire."

"Sell out?" Edward heard his own voice.

"We might get lucky." The chap squinted towards the head of the queue but it was out of sight.

Edward began to sweat. What if he couldn't get enough tickets, what if he couldn't get any?

Little by little they started shuffling forwards until, with relief, it was Edward's turn to step up to the ticket booth.

"Phew!" he said to the lady behind the counter. "I didn't think I'd get in."

She smiled kindly at him, her face framed by mint and lemon feathers.

"No need to worry, Sir. There's plenty of space. We'll make sure everyone gets in. Is it just the one ticket?"

"Actually, I'd like three please, you see I have an important business meeting and I promised to leave a ticket for the other business person behind the desk, would that be okay?"

"My pleasure, Sir."

She counted out the tickets and handed him an envelope.

"Are you taking the other two with you?" she asked.

"Oh no, the other one is for my au... I mean my assistant but she's running late, can I leave it here as well?"

"Absolutely, have another envelope."

As he wrote on the front of the envelope, he started to worry that the mint and lemon lady might say something to Claudette.

"The only thing is, when my assistant arrives can you not mention anything, you see she doesn't take well to being called an assistant and she might get cross and not come," he grinned at the kindly lady, realising he sounded a little silly.

"Certainly, Sir. I quite understand. I won't mention a thing to either party," she winked knowingly at him.

"Thank you," he winked back.

Walking through the entrance, Edward arrived among the stalls. The aroma of all the goodies; popcorn, toffee apples, chips, burgers, hot dogs, milkshakes and ice cream made him drool as punters walked past, digging into their purchases.

Gary and Barry strolled by, but with their arms full of popcorn and hot dogs, they failed to see him. He also dodged the Grouchers as they bumbled towards him. He needn't have worried; they were too busy arguing to notice him. Edward pulled his cap down in case he bumped into someone else and, straight away, bumped into someone.

"Ow!" Mrs Cabbage cried as he trod on her toe.

"Sorry Mrs Cabbage, you startled me."

"What took you so long?" she snapped. "We're running out of time. Come with me."

Edward followed as she quickly led him through the stalls to the side of the tent where it was much quieter. A huge field lay in front of him where a puppy bounced about, chasing its tail. Spotting Mrs Cabbage, the puppy raced over, yapping protectively.

"It's okay, Harriet, it's me!"

Edward noticed the change in Mrs Cabbage's voice straight away. She sounded like a child.

"Mrs Cabbage-" he began to say.

"Look over there," she interrupted him, pointing to the back of the tent.

A figure in a bright blue boiler suit was cartwheeling. Edward couldn't believe his eyes. Although he was some way off, he immediately knew he'd found his brother. Overjoyed, he started to walk towards him.

"Stop!" she hissed. "What are you doing?"

"I want to talk to him!" Edward said desperately.

"I said you could see him! Why do you want to talk to him?" Cucumber knew things were about to go horribly wrong.

"He's my brother!" Edward almost shouted.

"Okay, okay!" Cucumber knew there was no point arguing. "Stay there and I'll get him."

As she ran towards Nicky, she pulled the scarf from her head, uncovering her black, glossy hair. Then she stopped and stepped out of the brown skirt. She, like Nicky, was wearing a boiler suit covered in glittering stones and as she neared his brother, Edward realised she wasn't an old lady, she was a child!

Nicky listened intently before looking over to where Edward was waiting. Seconds later he was flinging himself into his brother's arms.

"Ed, Ed, I can't believe it, how did you find me, oh Ed I'm so sorry, I've been so stupid…I thought I was all alone but you're here…"

"Nicky!" Cassie's voice rang out from the other side of the tent.

"I'm here Cassie, just got carried away," he shouted back and then turning to Edward, whispered. "Wait there I'll be back in a minute."

Nicky sprinted back to where Edward had first seen him and once more started cartwheeling backwards and forwards. While he waited, Edward played with Harriet until Nicky returned.

"Cassie's gone for tools, I've only got a minute, I need to escape Ed. I don't know what they're planning but I overheard Mrs M say she wants to make me disappear after th-"

"Mrs M?" Edward interrupted. "What's she got to do with anything?"

"Don't you see Ed, she's the ringleader, she's the one in charge. They call her The Boss! I can't tell you how worried I've been, but Bernard and Aunty H have been really kind. Bernard's the one I have to help."

Nicky began to cry as the emotion he'd been holding in came flooding out.

"Hey Nicky, don't get upset. Everything will be fine." Edward placed a reassuring arm around his shoulders. "I'll rescue you."

"But how?" Nicky sniffed.

"I have a plan but there isn't time to tell you now," he ruffled Nicky's hair. "You'd better get back before you're missed, leave the rest to me."

The boys hugged and then Nicky dashed off, Harriet

happily chasing after him.

From outside the tent, Edward could hear the noise inside growing and realised people were taking their seats. With the show fast approaching, Edward began digging in his rucksack, pulling out his next disguise. A disguise, he hoped, that would even fool his mother.

The previous year she'd dressed as a cowboy for Nicky's birthday party and the wig she'd worn (black, fairly short and itchy), was perfect. Over the top of this, he popped on a sailor's cap, and to complete the look, a navy pilot's jacket. He decided the doctor's coat and vampire teeth probably wouldn't work with the overall effect and stuffed them back into the rucksack. Rolling up the sleeves of the jacket, he picked a couple of daisies and popped them in the lapel. Then he gazed at his feet and wiggled his toes. He'd never seen a businessman without shoes and was sure his mother hadn't either.

Taking Nicky's clean pants from the bottom of his rucksack he wrapped them around his feet, at least they were a dark colour and once inside the tent might pass for shoes.

Finally, he reached in and pulled out the small compact mirror and eyebrow pencil he'd taken from his mother's make-up bag. Then steadily he drew on a rather elaborate moustache.

"How do you do, Wing Commander Importante!" he said to his reflection. "Chocks away!"

And with that, he headed for the entrance, ticket in hand.

Chapter Twenty One

Backstage

Mrs M burst from the tent.

"Come in everyone!" she yelled and spotting Bernard, a newspaper covering his face as he snoozed in a deckchair, added. "For goodness sakes, wake him up!"

Then she disappeared back inside.

Nicky gently placed his hand on the old man's shoulder. "Bernard! Psst! Bernard!"

"What? What? How about a nice cup of tea?" he

blinked. "Ah Nicky, my dear boy, are you ready?"

"As I'll ever be!" he forced a smile. "Mrs M wants us to go in."

"Is it that time already? Right-O! Now there's something important I need to tell you, now what was it?" Bernard's eyebrows waggled up and down as he tried to remember. "Ah! Yes! That's it! What a silly old chap I am. Nicky, now you see the bright blue gemstone on your shoulder?"

Nicky looked sideways, he hadn't noticed before, but there was a disc-shaped button; it glittered and instinctively he raised his hand.

"No, no, Nicky, you mustn't touch it. Do you remember I told you I put magic in the costume?"

Nicky nodded.

"Well, I'm sure we won't need that kind of magic but, if we do," his voice was serious, "you must press it as hard as you can. Can you remember that?"

"Yes," Nicky replied, matching Bernard's serious tone. "But what does it do?"

Bernard started to make his way towards the tent.

"Now, you must promise me, you won't touch it unless I tell you to."

"I promise, but what does it do?" he pleaded.

"Let's hope you never find out." Bernard turned towards the little boy and winked. "Don't forget Cassie's signal and it'll be fine. Come on, young man, mustn't keep The Boss waiting."

Bernard pulled back the heavy material of the performers' entrance and they stepped in.

Backstage the atmosphere crackled with electricity as the cast bustled back and forth. Nicky noticed the older people were no longer hunched over, they walked tall and with ease, occasionally vaulting over a box or chair blocking their path. It was magical. Fairy lights strung from the material of the tent created sparkling shadows against the fabric.

Those getting ready stood close to the lights or used torches to apply make-up in front of large mirrors placed on the floor. Others stretched tights up legs and some stitched last-minute sequins onto their costumes. Despite the lack of light, everyone busily got on with what they needed to do.

On the other side of the curtain, Nicky could hear the audience taking their seats, the noise from their chatter fuelling his excitement as a wave of adrenaline swept through his body. Bernard nudged him and nodded towards a box in the furthest corner of the backstage area as Mrs M sprung onto it. There was no need to alert the other performers of her presence, they quietened immediately as she swept her arms dramatically and looked down her nose at the assembled troupe.

Wearing a black dressing gown with her lips painted a deep red, Nicky thought she looked evil. The power in her voice as she shouted above the noise of the crowd outside made him shudder.

"Ladies and gentlemen, boys and girls, the show's about to begin. As you know we've worked hard and I know this will be an incredible night."

Her eyes swept the room. "You are professionals, masters of your art. Be proud and show these people we're not too old and past it, nor are we too little or young!"

Again, she cast her steely gaze over the performers, coming to rest on Cassie.

"The 'accident' was unfortunate but only happened as a result of a lack of concentration. We must not repeat this!"

Cassie looked uncomfortable and her chin wobbled. Mrs M took her eyes from the young girl and flicked her head in Nicky's direction, blasting him with her full attention.

"Luckily for us, young Master Nicky has volunteered to step in. We are very grateful to you, but remember Nicky, you must concentrate, and above all, you must not let us down!"

Nicky nodded.

"Any questions?" she barked.

The room was silent.

"Good, then all that's left to say is, break a leg!" and with that, she leapt from the box.

Nicky watched as she strode across the tent and swooped behind a trunk, pulling Cucumber out. The little girl tried to back away, but Mrs M had her cornered and was talking directly into her face. Cucumber looked scared as Mrs M's finger wagged up and down. Nicky swallowed, remembering what Cassie had said about Cucumber always sneaking around, making things up, she'd definitely done something naughty!

Mrs M stalked off and the little girl screwed her face up, trying to hold back tears. Nicky felt sorry for her. When they'd first met, she'd been standoffish and rude but then, when she'd pointed towards Edward, he'd changed his mind.

Aunty H appeared and put an arm around the little girl and then, seeing Nicky, blew him a kiss. Catching it, Nicky popped it in his mouth and blew one back just as the lights dimmed.

Chapter Twenty Two
The Business Meeting

As Edward walked through the giant entrance tunnel, he filled his nostrils with the woody, fresh aroma of the sawdust covering the floor. Pushed along by the swarming crowd, he reached the main tent and his mouth gaped.

In front, they had constructed row after row of benches, one higher than the other forming semi-circles that towered over the performance area. Covered in black velvet, they held plush golden cushions for each bottom and, tucked underneath, furry black blankets to keep legs warm.

Gazing upwards, the height and size of the tent amazed him, making him feel like an ant. The fabric of the ceiling fell in deep swathes and was covered with tiny twinkling stars. Suspended from this hung a variety of ropes, swings and trapeze bars while the deep black velvet walls held flaming torches which cast a dramatic, fiery light. He'd never seen anything like it and was transfixed by its splendour.

In the centre sat several ramps and an enormous trampoline and for a while, all he could do was stare. It was spectacular. Then he remembered he needed to find his mother and, walking to the top of the first flight of stairs, began scanning the crowd.

It didn't take long to spot Gary and Barry in the front row, busily chatting. A few rows behind he spotted Claudette, her face illuminated by one of the multi-coloured spotlights which hung from the ceiling and cast rainbow beams into the crowd. She looked hypnotised as she shovelled large handfuls of popcorn towards her face, occasionally missing her mouth. A thin stringy man sat down on the seat next to her and they began talking. Twisting her head in his direction, she offered him some popcorn. Edward couldn't believe his luck, whoever this chap was, he and Claudette were getting along famously.

To the left, he could see Mr and Mrs Groucher talking animatedly, for once they weren't arguing.

The seats filled up as Edward continued searching for his mother. He'd taken his glasses off so she wouldn't recognise him but fearful he'd never spot her, he popped them on again. He leant forward to check the rows below but wobbled, suddenly reminded of the precarious situation he'd been in earlier. Steadying himself to avoid toppling into the lap of the lady in front, he took his seat just as the speakers sprung into life.

Music filled the tent and the last few stragglers rushed in keen to avoid missing the start of the show. Edward had just given up hope of finding his mother when, bursting through the curtains, she appeared.

He leapt to his feet and rushed down the stairs but, forgetting the sock-pants, almost skidded to the bottom. Slowing his pace, he waved enthusiastically until she spotted him and then, remembering his glasses, stuffed them in his pocket while she tripped daintily up to meet him. When she was only a few feet away, he took his hat off and bowed but the wig slipped forwards over his eyes. Swiftly he returned the hat to his head, pushing the hairpiece back into position and they shook hands vigorously.

"Mrs Dealer," he said in the deepest voice he could manage. "It is the greatest of pleasures to meet you. Please allow me to show you to your seat. I believe the show is about to begin."

He gestured for her to go first.

"It is a pleasure to meet you too, Mr Importante," Mrs Dealer replied as they took their seats.

Ferreting in her bag she pulled out an enormous bag of sweets and two toffee apples. Edward's eyes lit up.

"I have to admit, I can't resist these. Would you like one?" she smiled.

"Oh yes, please Moth…Mrs Dealer," he began in his usual high-pitched squeak but completed the sentence in Mr Importante's lower register. "It was a long flight and I haven't eaten yet."

Mrs Dealer paused for a moment and glanced sideways at him. She was sure she'd met him before?

"I thought on a private jet you would treat yourself to all kinds of goodies?" she enquired.

"Oh, I do Mrs Dealer, but when piloting it's best to keep both hands on the steering wheel!" he laughed jovially.

"I must admit I'm intrigued by your business proposition," she said, trying to move the conversation along.

"I hope you are Mrs Dealer. I was just coming to that."

Edward hadn't really had time to come up with a sensible idea, so instead, he rammed the toffee apple into his mouth and took an enormous bite.

"Sorry, just a moment," he said, trying to avoid spraying her with toffee and apple.

She looked away discreetly, giving him the opportunity to finish his mouthful. Edward chewed as slowly as he could.

"Delicious," another chew. "Mmm."

He'd nearly finished and knew he couldn't get away with stalling for much longer when…

The torches went out, the spotlights shut off, and the entire tent fell into total darkness. The audience was silent, all except Mrs Dealer.

"By the way, I think a trampoline would be a wonderful present for your nephew. I've been wondering about getting one for my son," she whispered.

Edward gave himself a high five in his head and was about to reply when a loud clap of thunder erupted and a flash of lightning streaked across the arena making the crowd gasp. Another rumble and then an ear-splitting

BOOM!

A powerful beam of brilliant white light illuminated a

spot in the middle as smoke billowed across the floor.

Unseen by the audience, a trapdoor opened and slowly, head bowed, a figure dressed in black emerged through the plumes of creeping smoke.

Drumming rumbled through the arena as the figure rose higher and higher into the air until it stopped and slowly raised its head.

Before he could stop himself, Edward blurted out incredulously. "Oh! My! Days!"

Mrs Dealer glanced sideways. What a peculiar little man, she thought.

Mrs M was the picture of evil with her black silky top hat and tails, a malevolent look on her face.

"You…" her voice rang out around the arena, "will experience the most jaw-dropping," she paused and scanned the audience with her piercing eyes, "the most awe-inspiring," she paused again for dramatic effect and turned her attention to the other side of the tent, "the most scintillating night of your lives!"

The audience cheered loudly.

"Be prepared for thrills and spills, triumphs and terror, shocks and surprises," she pointed her finger. "If you are of a nervous disposition, leave now!"

A couple with a small child began shuffling towards the

exit, trying to hide their embarrassment.

"If you bite your nails," screamed the voice. "Beware, you may not have any left by the time you leave!"

Then in the most sinister and ominous tone, she yelled, "You have been warned!"

Another almighty **BOOM!**

A **PUFF** of smoke.

And she vanished.

The audience, most of whom had moved to the edge of their seats, shuffled back to avoid falling off.

Chapter Twenty Three
The Show Begins

A soft glow appeared from the top of the tent as small globes of light floated down, pulsating like jellyfish. Human forms emerged from the shadows clothed completely in black and, taking the luminous balls, threw them through the air. They sent them high enough to touch the fabric of the ceiling and caught them as they sped towards the ground.

The graceful display mesmerised the crowd and, as it progressed in intensity and complexity, left them almost hypnotised. As the tempo of the music increased so did the flight of the balls and the excitement of the crowd until suddenly and dramatically, they merged into one.

The enormous globe floated above the audience, radiating an intense heat that spread across them. Then suddenly it flashed, exploding into thousands of tiny glittering stars which fell into the palms of the waiting audience. They sparked and fizzed, forming tiny gemstones which were quickly pocketed and the tent once more returned to darkness.

Soft lights went up, illuminating the central stage in pastel shades and the smell of baking bread, pastries, and fresh coffee filled the tent. Mrs S shuffled in balancing crockery on her Zimmer frame dressed in a flouncy tea lady outfit, causing some in the audience to scratch their heads. Surely it was too early for the intermission?

Poles had been set up around the arena and a tea party arranged on a table in the middle. Mrs S helped herself to a cup of tea and, having taken a sip, balanced it on top of a pole. She spun it and then raced back to the table for a plate of sandwiches; her speed astonished the audience. She selected a sandwich and took a bite before placing it back on the plate and then dashed across to another pole and spun that too!

She worked quickly, tasting and offering treats to the

audience. The crowd had been totally fooled, she was a skilled plate spinner, and to their delight, everything stayed in place. By the time she'd finished, there were fifty cups, saucers, bowls and plates all spinning at the same time.

The crowd showed their appreciation by applauding loudly as she dashed around, returning everything to the trolley. Then she threw her hands in the air and bowed before turning to the backstage curtain and whistling loudly.

Nine dogs trotted out and sat in two neat lines facing the audience. Each received a treat from the tea party before Mrs S shuffled backstage to more delighted cheers.

Music blared as Mr G and the Doggy Daredevils came bursting through the curtains. Dancing and clapping, he encouraged the audience to get on their feet and join him. Everyone wiggled along in time to the music as the dogs jumped and jived, flipped, flew, and pranced. The display charmed the crowd as they cheered the dogs' performance, but eventually, Mr G encouraged them to take their seats for the final routine. The doggy pyramid! Balancing on top of one another it was nearly perfect but for one dog which was missing, the one who should be at the top.

Mr G studied them and then, theatrically scratched his chin as though wondering what to do. He mimed counting them and then shook his head before placing his fingers in his mouth. He belted out an ear-piercing whistle and the cutest little puppy came bounding into the arena; it was Harriet!

The 'ahhh' which came for the audience made Harriet stop for a moment and a few people giggled; she really was adorable. Then she spotted Mr G and raced over to him, her tail wagging madly. He patted her and then gestured towards the other dogs. Harriet, tail still wagging, trotted up to the pyramid and sprung to the top.

Standing on her hind legs, she waved her front paws in the air until a signal from Mr G had her jumping down. The others followed and then Mr G ordered them into a line and they bowed. The crowd applauded their exit enthusiastically.

The acts that followed amazed and wowed the audience; fabulous fire breathing by Mr A, tightrope walking by Mr D, hula hooping by Mrs D and sword swallowing by Mrs G. They were hard pushed to pick a favourite as each act was more astounding than anything they'd seen before. Even Mrs Dealer (who'd seen thousands of acts throughout her career) was in awe. She clapped, cheered and whooped her way through the rest of the performance. At one point Edward was quite surprised when she raised her hands to her mouth and blasted out a whistle of appreciation.

Backstage, Cucumber peered out from a tiny gap in the curtains. Since her brief conversation with Mrs M, she'd been avoiding her and was petrified she'd get collared again.

Sitting in the tree, only a day ago, she'd wanted to find out what was going on, but it seemed like a long time ago and lots had happened since. When Edward read her the newspaper article about the missing child, she'd worried, wondering whether Mrs M had something to do with Georgia May George. Then when Mrs M had caught her at the start of the show, she'd told her she knew she'd been spying on them and wanted to know what she'd been up to. She was in the worst trouble of her life.

"So, Cucumber, trying to avoid me? You can't do that for the rest of your life, can you?"

The little girl froze, the voice was only millimetres from her ear and she could feel the heat rising, spreading across her cheeks and down her neck.

"I trust you've had time to think about what I said?"

Cucumber turned and tried to step back, but Mrs M grabbed her arm tightly, refusing to let go.

"P-p-please Mrs M, y-y-you're hurting me," the little girl winced with pain and tried to twist her arm free. Mrs M loosened her grip slightly.

"I want to know what you've been up to, it's time you

spilt those beans," and with a flourish, The Boss pulled the picture diary from behind her back. Cucumber gulped.

"It's nothing Mrs M, it's j-j-just my p-p-picture diary…"

Mrs M glowered. "It's not 'nothing'," she said menacingly. "Everything you've been up to is in these pages. Did you really think you could sneak about unseen? That no one would notice you hanging about in the tree?"

"I always hang about!" the little girl replied honestly.

"At Apple Blossom Crescent? You know you're not allowed outside the hospital grounds. We have to keep everything secret and there you are just wandering across town like nothing matters!"

Sensibly, Cucumber didn't reply. Most people knew her in town, as did all the bus drivers. She couldn't help having an adventurous spirit, she thought.

"Where is he, Cucumber?"

Cucumber tried to remain calm.

"If Nicky's brother ruins this because you've filled his head with some ridiculous, childish idea of yours, then there's no telling what will happen."

"I haven't!" Cucumber continued to stare at Mrs M, desperately trying to blink away tears.

"You are so irresponsible!" snarled Mrs M. The guilt on Cucumber's face was visible. "Don't you realise what you've done. If our plan goes wrong it'll be your fault!"

Cucumber couldn't believe her ears.

"My fault?" hissed the little girl, suddenly seeing red. "How, of all people, can you say any of this is my fault?"

Mrs M stepped back, surprised and confused by her reaction.

"Whatever do you mean?" she asked.

"I mean I was there, the day you knocked the chairs on Cassie, the day you messed things up. It's your fault, not mine!" Hot tears of rage streamed down her face.

It was Mrs M's turn to feel guilty.

Cucumber couldn't stop herself, "and then you got a stranger in to take the starring role. What about me? You never asked me! It's all I've ever dreamt of!" she wept.

Mrs M continued to stare, rarely was she lost for words.

Cucumber snatched her arm out of Mrs M's grip.

"And I know about the newspaper article," she folded her arms across her body, waiting for a reaction.

Luckily, Aunty H appeared.

"What are you two up to?"

She stood between them.

"We haven't got time for this, Bernard's on, you need to take your places!"

Mrs M stormed off and Cucumber began to tremble as

Aunty H hugged her tightly.

"Cucumber!" she heard Cassie's whispered command in the dark. "We're on!"

Bat

Chapter Twenty Four
Where the Magic Happens

Darkness so black they couldn't see their hands in front of their faces meant the audience could only guess where the middle of the arena was. Patiently and nervously they waited for something to happen.

After a while, a few in the top row started to shudder as a strange sensation tickled the back of their necks. It sent shivers up and down their spines and they murmured to one another trying to seek reassurance. It wasn't long before the entire audience was tingling and itching uncomfortably in their seats. At the top of the tent a faint glow appeared but being far too unsettled, most didn't spot it. Then, a little girl in the front row cried out.

"I'm scared, Mummy! There's a bat in here!"

A spotlight illuminated her and everyone turned to where the child pointed. There was a dark shadow in the middle of the arena. Slowly, their eyes grew accustomed to the dark, and a figure emerged. Clothed in a deep purple velvet cape, face obscured by a hood, it took flight. Flying through the audience, a few ducked as it approached, while others shivered at the touch that lifted their hair when it glided over the top of their heads.

Eventually, it stopped its attack and landed gracefully in the middle of the arena. Crouching low, it rose to its feet and elegantly walked like a dancer, toes pointing forwards, towards the frightened child. The child shrank into her seat but the figure didn't stop and as it approached, raised its hand over her head.

Every single person held their breath, even the little girl's parents froze, too fearful to move.

The child wiggled her bottom back, but as she did her expression changed, from fear to awe, and then to wonder. Waves of glitter fell from the outstretched hand. Red then blue then green, then pink and yellow and purple. The little girl gazed upwards as she began to laugh. Glitter landed on the end of her nose. The figure spoke softly, and she nodded before sticking out her tongue.

"Strawberry!" she giggled.

The hooded figure tilted its head to one side as though asking the audience whether they wanted to share the experience.

"Yes!" shouted Garry.

"And me!" yelled Barry.

And before they knew it, glitter was snowing down on them.

"Pineapple," said Mrs Dealer to Edward.

"Mine tastes of bubble gum," he replied, smiling up at her.

The figure turned and walked to the centre of the arena and then, without warning, a golden cloud appeared and showers of gold and silver rained down.

The hood of the cloak fell.

"Hello, my delightful friends," said the rainbow glitter magician. his voice echoing around the tent. "My name is Bernardo the Most Mysterious and Marvellous Magician; it is so wonderfully wonderful to have you all here tonight."

The crowd clapped and cheered, and some that remembered him from long ago cried tears of joy.

"It's been a long time since I've stood amongst you, too long and I've missed you, each and every one of you."

Again, cheers and applause.

"As has my wonderful assistant, the enchanting and beguiling, Henrietta!"

He raised his right hand, fingers outstretched towards the top of the tent where a beautiful bird was gracefully gliding to the ground. Once she'd landed, Aunty H curtsied, and the crowd erupted with delight.

"My most special assistant has many talents, too many to show you today, but we promise to astound you. Some of you may think we can't do it anymore but I assure you, we can!"

Bernardo treated the audience to an amazing display of magic, as Aunty H cartwheeled, somersaulted and backflipped throughout the entire routine. He sawed her in half, sending sections of her body flying off in different directions, shot bullets and knives at her and even, at one point, had her in a birdcage which she escaped from. Then, it was time for her to fly away and Bernardo continued by making doves, butterflies and tropical birds appear from his hands. They swooped around the tent and landed chirping and fluttering in the audience, much to their delight. He even performed levitation tricks on members of the audience, dazzling and confusing them in equal measure.

Finally, just as the crowd didn't think it could get any better, the lights dimmed and Bernardo rose into the air.

He spoke warmly. "And now my wonderful friends, time for the finale."

Edward still hadn't spotted his brother and began to worry.

Bernardo continued, "I will ask my dear friends, the Flaming Cycles for some assistance, please excuse me, I have some business to attend to in the sky!" and with that, he flew to the top of the tent, remaining in shadow next to a golden hoop.

Chapter Twenty Five

The Finale

Once more, darkness enveloped the audience as a rumbling sensation vibrated up their legs into their bottoms. Then the sudden roar of engines made some spring from their seats in surprise, only to sit again as the curtains opened.

A blinding white light and smoke meant it was difficult to see until the Flaming Cycles screeched through, skidding into the middle of the arena.

Standing on top of their bike seats, all nine bowed and then, jumping back down into their saddles, began weaving through one another, just as they had when Nicky first met them.

Some raced up ramps secured to the staircase and started swooping around the back of the audience, and as the one in yellow passed, Edward waved. Mrs Cabbage flew past several times before she recognised him and her bike swerved.

Fireworks jetted into the air as the final bike glided into the arena and Edward watched Nicky, sitting on top of the rider's shoulders, wave to the audience. Pride and fear swept through his body in equal measure as Cassie carefully guided Nicky to the centre where he backflipped off her shoulders onto the trampoline.

He began bouncing straight away.

At the top of the tent, Bernardo swooped through the hoop he'd been hovering next to and it burst into flames. He took a dove from his pocket and it took flight. Bernardo clicked his fingers, and the dove returned to him. It had to pass through the hoop to get to him and as it did, vanished completely.

Below, the ten bikes continued to perform tricks as they waited for Nicky's bounces to be high enough and then split into two groups on either side of the trampoline. As he backflipped, cartwheeled and somersaulted the crowd stared unblinkingly, not wanting to miss a single bounce. By now he was catapulting high into the sky and finally, Cassie signalled to the others.

Two bikes came from opposite sides racing up the ramps, passing underneath Nicky as he reached the top of his bounce.

Through Nicky's visor, Edward could see the strain on his brother's face and squeezed the edge of the bench, his knuckles white. To distract himself, he dragged his gaze to where Bernardo hovered in the shadows. The fire around the hoop was burning brightly, the magician's face visible briefly from the light it cast. All eyes were on Nicky and the bikes but not Edward's, no, his eyes were on the magician. Something wasn't right.

He looked back at his brother getting nearer and nearer the flames and then over to Bernardo, at his head tilted oddly to one side.

Fear overwhelmed Edward as the flames leapt and danced. Nicky was getting dangerously close and his eyes darted once more to Bernardo. He knew, straight away, what was wrong. Bernardo had fallen asleep!

No!

Edward was on his feet racing around the back of the crowd as Nicky continued to journey closer and closer to the flames, sweat now dripping from his forehead.

Mrs Dealer stared at the vacant seat next to her. Really, she thought, this Mr Importante was a most unusual character!

Edward dashed to the steps and launched himself at the nearest trapeze ladder. Taking it in both hands, he looked up as it stretched above, going on forever. He gulped and his heart raced as he placed one foot on the first rung. Knowing he had no head for heights, his legs shook violently as fear, once more, raced through his body. His arms were wobbling too, and the ladder lurched from side to side as he scrambled upwards.

At the halfway point he stopped for a moment, trying to catch his breath and glanced over to where Nicky was still bouncing. He turned his attention to Bernardo, but he was still asleep and so, with a renewed sense of urgency, he scrambled upwards. So focused on his goal, Edward didn't even realise his shoe-pants were unravelling.

With all eyes mesmerised by the display below no one had noticed the small boy, dressed as a pilot, clambering up but that was about to change. In the wings, Mrs M had noticed the jerky movement of the ladder and following it up, spotted him. Her eyes narrowed, and she sprang into action, covering the distance in long balletic leaps.

Edward felt the ladder swing as the weight of Mrs M pulled it from side to side like a boat on dangerous water. He saw her coming at a great rate of knots like a gigantic wave that would engulf him and tried to take another step. His foot slipped as one of the shoe-pants finally came loose, dangling on the end of his toe until he shook it free.

Some in the crowd noticed the commotion and didn't know where to look. Nicky was about to reach the hoop but on the other side, they could see Mrs M and a pilot. What on earth was going on?

Some saw the underwear float down and land on top of Mrs M's head, a few chuckled as she tried unsuccessfully to remove it.

Edward reached the top and glanced down again. He was now less afraid of heights and more afraid of the shark that was pursuing him. He could almost feel her breath on the back of his neck as he extended his arm to grab the trapeze bar. Wrapping his fingers around the cool metal he swung backwards before launching forwards.

"**AAAAGGGGGHHHHHH!**" he screamed as a weight slammed heavily onto his back.

Swinging through the air he glanced at his hands, they weren't the only ones gripping the bar and so he turned and stared straight into the eyes of the monster behind him.

Mrs Dealer, who'd been following Mr Importante's progress, smiled wryly. She'd been duped before but never so spectacularly. I get it, she thought, Mr Importante was an imposter, he was a performer who'd invited her along, so she'd offer to act as their entertainment agent.

The crowd loved the spectacle and, as it raced towards its conclusion, began to roar and shriek. The riders backflipped and twisted as they raced under Nicky, using the space between jumps until Cassie stopped, and moved into position. By now, Nicky was red-faced and visibly panting.

A spotlight cast its beam on Cassie while the others moved to the side. The audience began a steady hand clap as she signalled to the boy on the trampoline. She pushed off, gaining speed and reached the ramp just as Nicky hurtled back down, feet first.

On the trapeze, Mrs M had dragged herself up and now stood with her feet on the bar whilst Edward dangled below. It had only been a few seconds, but to Edward, it seemed like hours.

Cassie and the bike soared upwards as Nicky landed feet first on her shoulders and they hit the trampoline together before being catapulted into the air. Nicky's feet left the rider's shoulders and continued on his upward journey while Cassie skidded to a halt on the ground below.

"Bernardo, Bernardo!" Edward screamed repeatedly as his helpless brother flew above him.

Nicky rocketed towards the hoop just as Mrs M made one final leap. Arms outstretched like an eagle she soared over the top of him, he could hear her yelling but didn't have a clue what she was saying above the shrieks coming from the audience. She looked most peculiar, hurtling towards the hoop, slapping her right shoulder violently.

BOOM!

And she'd gone!

Rainbow stars filled the tent, shooting left, right, up and raining down on the audience below.

Nicky suddenly realised what Mrs M was doing, she was telling him he was in danger. As he sailed through the hoop, his arm shot to his shoulder and he thumped where he thought the blue disc was, remembering what Bernard had told him. There was magic in the costume and he needed it!

Dramatically, his body soared upwards as the wings which Bernard had stitched into the boiler suit took him zig-zagging around the top of the tent. He narrowly avoided flying through the fabric before soaring straight back towards the ground. Looking down at the audience, their faces getting closer, he'd just started to panic when someone grabbed hold of his hand. Bernardo, woken by all the commotion, had come to his rescue and the pair did one final loop of the arena before landing gracefully.

As they stood, facing the audience, Bernardo held the little boy tightly and whispered gently to him, "It's okay Nicky, you're safe now."

Way up above, Edward was so relieved he forgot where he was and took one hand off the trapeze bar to wipe the sweat now pouring down his face. Then he realised, for the second time that day, he was holding on with one hand whilst being a great distance from the ground. He scrabbled desperately, trying to grab the bar, but his palms were sweaty and his strength failing.

And then, he was falling.

Closing his eyes tightly he waited to hit the ground.

Chapter Twenty Six

Applause

The audience fell silent as the pilot plummeted.

Down, down he dropped, arms and legs scrabbling desperately as he tried to catch thin air.

Holding their breath, they were all hoping for a miracle.

Fortunately, one came.

A motorbike screeched into the arena, Cucumber in full command of the machine. Racing towards a ramp, both she and the bike launched into the air.

With Edward falling fast, she expertly angled herself so

that he landed, with a heavy thump, on the seat behind her. His body slumped forward over hers and they met the ground with a jolt. Controlling the bike as it jerked up and down and wobbled from side to side, Cucumber guided them back through the curtains to the backstage area.

The lights went up. The crowd erupted.

Backstage, Edward, still in a state of shock, barely noticed the mint bird lady drag him from the bike. She held him tightly while he trembled uncontrollably.

In the main tent the crowd continued to cheer and whoop, it was by far the best thing they'd ever seen. A few had fainted (the faint-hearted ones) so friends and relatives dug in their bags for something to revive them with.

The lights dimmed whilst the applause continued and the audience took their seats again.

Bernard and Nicky waited while the riders joined them. Spotlights illuminated their faces as they removed their helmets and the crowd realised, with astonishment, that children were smiling and waving back at them! The applause was deafening.

Another spotlight cast its beam onto the curtain as Mr Importante was led back into the arena, Aunty H supporting him. Mrs Dealer watched as he raised his head in wonder, gazing at the audience. The movement made both his wig and hat slip and they fell to the ground.

"Edward?" Mrs Dealer cried. "Could it possibly be?"

The lady sitting next to her gave her a funny look.

"I'm sorry, it's just that the boy with Henrietta reminds me of my eldest son." Her smile withered as she thought about how ridiculous she sounded.

Placing her glasses on the end of her nose she leant forward, she recognised the boy in the blue boiler suit too.

"Nicky!" she said, barely above a whisper.

"Is that your other son?" joked the lady, giving Mrs Dealer a pitying look.

"Yes!" was the stunned reply.

"And I guess your cleaning lady's down there too?" the lady laughed, thinking she was hilariously funny.

Mrs Dealer's face went ghostly white.

She continued to stare as Aunty H and Edward moved toward the other entertainers and the Flaming Cycles mounted their bikes. Then she saw Nicky race towards his brother and leap into his arms where they held each other tightly.

She needed no more proof and, although stunned, was desperate to get to her boys. With the audience already leaving, blocking the stairs, she started clambering over the benches in front. Some still contained seated people but oblivious to their cries of 'Oi!' and 'Mind where you're going!' she mountaineered down.

On the other side of the arena, the penny had dropped with Claudette too who was equally keen to get to the boys. Her descent not as ladylike as Mrs Dealer's as she saw her job, home, and uninterrupted hours in front of the television, slipping through her fingers.

In her haste she lost her footing and started rolling down the benches, gathering speed and taking people out as she tumbled. She landed with a crash, face first on the sawdust. She wasn't down for long though. Edward turned just in time to see her charging towards them like a bull.

Unfortunately, Mrs Dealer hadn't seen and was knocked down like a skittle as Claudette bowled into her. Bernard swiftly moved towards the women, helping Claudette to her feet while the boys flung themselves at their mother.

"I think you'd better follow me," he said politely but firmly.

In the audience, Gary's mother had to physically shut his open mouth while Mr and Mrs Groucher began arguing about whether the two main performers were the funny little Dealer boys that lived across the road.

Chapter Twenty Seven
Explanations

Mrs Dealer sat in the middle of the comfiest sofa clinging onto Edward and Nicky. By their side, Claudette perched on the edge, biting her nails.

Bernard stood in the middle of the room. Although he was anxious, he appeared calm to the eight eyes that followed him, each waiting for an explanation.

Taking a deep breath, he began.

"Ladies, please allow me to ask you a simple question,"

His charming smile slipped and his eyes narrowed. "Can either of you tell me where these boys have been for the last couple of days?"

Both remained silent until Claudette whispered, "The library?"

"The library!" Mrs Dealer glared at the au pair. "Surely not all the time?"

"Well, erm…" Claudette's voice trailed off.

Bernard grinned at the boys. "Then I think it is safe to say you are unaware that these fine chaps have helped us put on the best performance of our lives!"

Mrs Dealer and Claudette stared at the boys in stunned confusion.

"I think we'd better start at the beginning, don't you?" Bernard suggested.

Mrs Dealer and Claudette nodded in agreement.

"Us oldies were born into the circus and, when we were younger, travelled the world. We were famous back then and performed for years, moving from one place to the next. Age crept up on us and the travel became too much. We bought the old hospital intending to set up a permanent showground."

Aunty H continued. "We hadn't been here long when Mrs M found Colin, the eldest of the Flaming Cycles. She'd started a cleaning job to help with the money while we were getting ourselves sorted and one night, on her way home, heard a baby crying. There wasn't anyone about so she stuck him in her shopping trolley. He was a gorgeous little boy but hungry and his clothes were in an awful mess. We cleaned him up, fed him and loved him. All the time we scoured the papers and checked the news reports but weeks rolled by and there was no mention of him. No desperate parents, no relatives of any kind and no home for him to go to. We fell in love with him and that's when our unusual family was born."

She took a breath.

"A year later Mrs M found another one, our lovely Cassie. It was the same story with her, no one looked, no one came so we kept her too! I think you can guess what happened with the rest of the Flaming Cycles. It would appear Mrs M has a knack for accidentally finding babies!"

Bernard beamed with paternal pride before continuing.

"I even adapted her vacuum cleaner so it would suck them up, much easier for the old girl to bring them home."

Aunty H chuckled, "To be honest she could have carried them but she's not fond of babies and I think Bernard enjoyed inventing a child sucking vacuum cleaner, another of his vanishing tricks!"

Bernard smiled gratefully, "We realised quickly that we couldn't set the circus up, we had enough on our hands caring for the children and besides, we didn't want anyone sniffing about. We were afraid if anyone saw them, they'd say we were too old to look after them and take them away. There's no way we'd let that happen. We won't let anyone break up our family!"

Aunty H stepped in as Bernard's eyes began to water.

"We started training them a few years ago, for a bit of fun. We wanted to show them what we used to do and the whole thing's been a bit of a happy accident." Aunty H grinned with pride. "They're far better than we ever imagined. I'm sure you'll agree the Flaming Cycles are hugely talented."

The ladies nodded.

"However, time has passed incredibly quickly and caring for ten children can be expensive. Our savings have nearly gone and with only the money from Mrs M's cleaning jobs we've struggled. Especially with the old hospital. You can see it's crumbling and we can't afford the repairs."

"And that leads us to tonight," it was back to Bernard. "A few months ago, we came up with the idea for the show. A one-off so we could make enough money to move on. Something in the countryside where it's easier to keep ourselves to ourselves and with plenty of space for the children to play."

The ladies continued to nod.

"Everything had been going swimmingly until Cassie's accident. With only a few days to go, we needed a replacement." Bernard turned to Nicky. "Mrs M's been your cleaner for a while and had noticed you practising. She'd mentioned you a few times, even before we asked for your help. Thank you, my darling boy, from the bottom of my heart."

Tenderly he placed a hand on the little boy's face. "You are superbly talented, a born performer with a glittering career in front of you." Bernard winked at Nicky.

Nicky looked at them both. "I still don't understand," he said without smiling. "I heard Mrs M say she wanted to make me disappear." He shuddered. "It didn't sound nice."

"Oh, my little darling, don't you understand, that's exactly what we intended to do. If you'd reached the hoop before Mrs M that's exactly what would have happened, you'd have disappeared!"

She walked over and held his hand.

He looked at her, wanting to believe her. "Then what?"

"Mrs M planned to take you home while we packed up."

"Was that all?" he stared at the ground.

"Yes!" Aunty H replied in total amazement. "I'm so sorry Nicky, we never meant to frighten you. I can see we've been a bit too secretive, but it was only because we worry about the children. People will already be gossiping about them, wondering where they've come from and who they are."

Nicky blushed. "So, by the time I got home and told everyone about the show you'd have gone and no one would have been able to find you."

Things started to click into place. It explained why Cucumber had been so concerned about the police and why she'd assumed he'd come to live with them. He realised he'd been unbelievably stupid! When Mrs M said she was the ringleader, that's what she'd meant. The ringleader of a circus, not a criminal gang.

"It probably wasn't the best plan, but we hoped people wouldn't believe you."

Bernard smiled mischievously before turning to Edward.

"I must thank you. Your trapeze act saved your brother's life. You should be proud of yourself. I can't tell you how grateful we are."

"You mustn't thank me. I just wanted to help my brother," Edward replied.

"And you did, in a most marvellous way but I must ask, how did you find us? We thought we'd covered our tracks. Mrs M said you'd get the postcard and wait for Nicky to come home. She thought you'd enjoy the peace and quiet. I imagine looking after him can be a lot of work?"

Claudette reddened.

Edward grinned. "I don't mind, he's my brother, but the truth is I never read the postcard. Mrs Cabbage's puppy took a liking to it and destroyed it."

"Mrs Cabbage?" Bernard and Aunty H glanced at one another quizzically.

"Yes, the one who saved my life, I owe her a great deal, she's been very helpful. I wouldn't be here if it wasn't for her but when I met her at Apple Blossom Crescent, I thought she was an old lady. She dressed like one."

"Cucumber!" exclaimed Bernard and Aunty H at the same time.

"No, Cabbage!" Edward replied, correcting them as the old lady had done in his bedroom.

"There is no Mrs Cabbage," said Aunty H. "But there is a Cucumber, she's seven years old."

"Seven years old!" Edward already knew she was a child, but couldn't believe she was so young. However, it explained why she'd been able to run so fast, slide down bedsheets and flip over balconies. "But why did she come to Apple Blossom Crescent?"

Aunty H folded her arms. "Cucumber! I think you've got some explaining to do!"

The little girl stepped from behind a curtain. Everyone stared at her.

"I'm sorry." She stared at the floor. "I wanted to know why you were all being so secretive so I followed Mrs M to Apple Blossom Crescent. That's when Harriet ruined the postcard." She looked up, her dark eye brimming with tears. "And then I heard Mrs M and Bernard talking in the caravan, they said Edward would have seen the postcard but I knew he hadn't. It scared me, I thought he'd call the police and they'd take us away and it'd be my fault. I just wanted to be the star of the show, but all I've done is make a mess of everything!"

"Oh Cucumber," said Bernard. "You're already the star of the show, we couldn't have done it without you and the rest of the Flaming Cycles. Don't you understand, you're all as important as each other." He walked over to the little girl and enveloped her in a great big bear hug.

"So, what now?" asked Mrs Dealer. "What are you going to do?"

"I don't know," replied Bernard. "It depends on the

trouble we've got ourselves into. It depends on what you're planning to do, now you know?"

"You're not in any trouble! I won't tell anyone or do anything!" she replied.

"Really?" Bernard asked.

"Actually, no, that's not true. I will do something." Mrs Dealer stood. "I'll help you, if you're willing to let me."

Bernard looked quizzically at her.

"I'll help you sell the old hospital, get you set up somewhere else, I won't let anyone separate this amazing family!"

"You'd do that for us?" Bernard was almost speechless.

"My mother raised me in the circus, but as I grew up, I became embarrassed. Everyone else had 'normal' parents and 'normal' lives. I couldn't face telling my lovely Mum that I didn't want to follow in her footsteps so I made a decision, a terrible decision. I ran away." a tear slid down Mrs Dealer's face. "A few years later, having realised my mistake, I tried searching for her but it was as if she'd disappeared. I even set up Dealer & Sons in the hope she'd walk through my door one day."

Mrs Dealer smiled at Aunty H.

"I knew it was you when I collected the ticket but I was late and in shock. I'm sorry Mum. I have been trying to find you."

"Oh, my darling, I thought I'd never see you again, we've got a lot of catching up to do." Aunty H opened her arms wide, and they hugged.

"One more thing," Mrs Dealer said, releasing her mother and turning to Claudette. "Seeing as you are so rubbish at looking after the children, I think it's best we find something else for you to do!"

Claudette stared wide-eyed and nodded. "Yes, Mrs Dealer. I'm so sorry, I'll do anything!"

Bernard walked to the main door and as he opened it, the Flaming Cycles and the old folk tumbled into the room.

"Time for a celebration, fizzy pop for the children and maybe something stronger for the adults?"

Everyone cheered.

Chapter Twenty Eight
Happy Ever After?

No one saw Mrs M that evening but no one looked. They were too busy celebrating to notice and besides, she'd only dampen the mood. However, the next morning Cassie found a note and went straight to Bernard.

"Mrs M's gone!" she told him.

"What do you mean 'gone'," he replied, frowning at the young girl.

"Her caravan isn't here, and I found a note on her

dressing table in the tent."

She handed it to him.

Bernard read it and then sighed. "Oh well, it's for the best. We can all do with a break from her!"

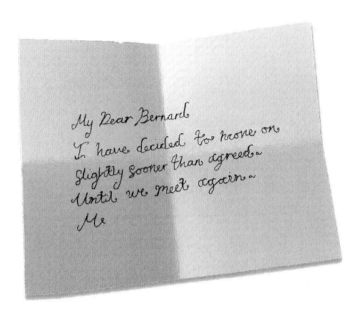

My Dear Bernard
I have decided to move on slightly sooner than agreed.
Until we meet again.
Me

Cassie stared at him in horror. "You can't say that!"

He laughed. "You know what she's like. She'll already be poking her nose into someone else's business. Don't worry, she'll turn up. In the meantime, let's enjoy our holiday and I promise we'll work something out when we get back, agreed?"

"Agreed!" said Cassie, skipping off to pack her suitcase.

A glorious week in Southend followed, full of sandcastle building, ice cream licking and sea swimming.

As soon as they returned, Mrs Dealer, being an efficient lady, set to work. She took over the sale of the old hospital and started searching for a house in the country where they could set up a permanent showground. She hadn't forgotten Nicky's birthday either and gave him a brand new trampoline, a rainbow coloured one. He didn't know whether to laugh or cry.

Aunty H didn't waste any time either. With two extra children to love and care for she couldn't believe her luck and with enthusiasm, doubled her knitting pace.

Edward and Bernard worked well together. A dedicated student, Edward soaked up every trick Bernard taught him while Nicky and Cucumber practised gymnastics with Cassie.

One lunchtime Bernard appeared with fried egg sandwiches for everyone. Nicky took one look and clamped his hand firmly over his mouth. Later, when his tummy stopped churning, he told Bernard about the hideous breakfast Mrs M had prepared.

To his surprise, Bernard started laughing. It began with a slow chortle but soon grew to an uncontrollable belly laugh. Nicky didn't understand and was on the verge of calling for help when Bernard stopped laughing long enough to explain.

"I haven't told you before, but Mrs M's my older sister," he spluttered between shakes.

Nicky grimaced at the idea.

"Well, she did the same to me when we were younger," by now he'd laughed so much he was hiccupping.

"And you think it's funny?" Nicky couldn't understand why Bernard found it so amusing.

"Not at the time I didn't," he grinned fondly at the memory. "You reckon I'm a great magician, but my sister is the real master of illusion."

"How?" he asked.

"She didn't put snot in your sandwich, it was lime marmalade but I hope you didn't try the lemon lump!" and with that, he fell about laughing again.

Nicky had to agree it was a good trick and made a mental note to play it on his brother.

"But why would she do something so horrible?"

"Nicky, my dear boy, did she see you picking your nose?" Bernard asked.

"Yes." Nicky grinned sheepishly.

"And have you picked it since?"

Nicky shook his head.

"Then you've learnt your lesson, just as I did. She really is a rotter!" he giggled, winking at the little boy.

As for Claudette, things worked out for her too. She became Mrs Dealer's assistant, and plans were made for her to take over the ticket office from Aunty H. She and Bernard were already creating a fantastic peacock themed costume which she couldn't wait to wear. She'd also arranged a date with the young man who she'd sat next to at the show.

A few weeks later, Bernard was reading the newspaper.

"Have you seen this about Georgia May George, H?" he asked.

"Not yet, dear." Aunty H was sitting in an armchair, eating cake.

"It says she's still missing and they haven't found the mysterious lady with the headscarf."

"And they won't," replied Cucumber.

Bernard looked at her. "What do you mean, Cucs?"

"Mrs M's long gone!" she replied, not quite believing Bernard hadn't worked it out.

"Mrs M! Why on earth would you think M had anything to do with it?"

"I worked it out when Edward read me the newspaper article in his bedroom. She must be involved, a woman wearing a headscarf and a disappearing child? How could it not be her?"

"Oh Cucumber, you're wrong!"

Edward, who was tickling Harriet's ear, looked up from his big Book of Magic.

"Bernard, I know she's your sister but you've got to admit it looks a little suspicious. Especially when you consider she slunk off into the night straight after the show."

"That doesn't prove she's got anything to do with it!"

"I have to admit, I wondered if Georgia May George was Cucumber but then I remembered you said you only found babies."

Bernard raised an eyebrow. "And I was telling the truth! Georgia May George and Cucumber aren't the same person!" Bernard turned to Cucumber. "Are you?"

"Absolutely not!" laughed Cucumber. "A small girl with short black hair, a pencil case and a satchel isn't that uncommon!"

"I know," replied Edward. "But I think there's a connection."

Edward took out a clipping out of his pocket. It was from a newspaper article he'd read a few days before.

"Here's a picture of Georgia May George. I think you'll

agree they look identical."

Bernard and Cucumber studied the image.

"It is a bit odd, I agree," he sighed.

"She looks like me!" Cucumber whispered.

"So, what shall we do?" Edward asked.

"About what?" Bernard knew he was about to agree to something he didn't want to.

"About finding Georgia May and Mrs M!"

Bernard groaned. "Why would we want to find them?"

"Because it's another disappearing act!" Edward exclaimed.

"But we don't know where to start!" said Bernard, desperately trying to come up with an excuse not to get involved.

Nicky turned to his brother. "Ed?"

"Oh, that's easy," he replied. "We start at the beginning!"

GOODBYE...
TILL NEXT
TIME...

Thank you

Like my characters, young, old and some in the middle have contributed and supported me in writing this. To you all a big thank you.

Demelza Knight, Corinne Harvey, Sarah Dunthorne, Wendy Kavanagh, Helen Robson, Sadie Vile, Abi Spence and Rachel Calkin. Thank you for your time, interest, and encouragement. You have all gone above and beyond in helping me put on the show.

To Linda and Michael Ambrose, I couldn't have done it without you. I love you both.

Thanks also to Miki and Grahame Marks. You have been a fantastic support, and it is my turn to say I am very lucky to have you.

Thanks also to everyone who has provided me with props, animals and oddities to photograph. Chrissie Absalom, Kelly Rickards, Rich & Fran Harris, Jackie Hannam, John Oakley, and Rob Knight (Captain of The Eastfield Intoxicated).

A huge round of applause for the Flaming Cycles in my life. None of them live in an old hospital nor do they ride motorbikes but they are, like my characters, super talented, courageous, funny and a joy to be around. Betsy, Minnie, Lydia, Stanley, Lottie, Daniel, Sophie, George, and Luke.

A great big cheer goes especially to Sam Knight and Caitlin Harvey, your feedback was 'amazing' and creative input superb!

A big whistle of appreciation goes to the Doggy Daredevils, Mali, Mabel, Sky, Simba, Jake, Cindy, Lara, Eva, Monty & Buddy, thank you.

To the stars of the show, Ava and Nicky, thank you for absolutely everything and more.

And finally, thanks to Pete, who I am relatively fond of.

Printed in Poland
by Amazon Fulfillment
Poland Sp. z o.o., Wrocław

53644811R00134